TARGET THREE

(THE SPY GAME—BOOK 3)

JACK MARS

Jack Mars

Jack Mars is the USA Today bestselling author of the LUKE STONE thriller series, which includes seven books. He is also the author of the new FORGING OF LUKE STONE prequel series, comprising six books; of the AGENT ZERO spy thriller series, comprising twelve books; of the TROY STARK thriller series, comprising five books; and of the SPY GAME thriller series, comprising six books.

Jack loves to hear from you, so please feel free to visit www.Jackmarsauthor.com to join the email list, receive a free book, receive free giveaways, connect on Facebook and Twitter, and stay in touch!

BOOKS BY JACK MARS

THE SPY GAME
TARGET ONE (Book #1)
TARGET TWO (Book #2)
TARGET THREE (Book #3)
TARGET FOUR (Book #4)
TARGET FIVE (Book #5)
TARGET SIX (Book #6)

TROY STARK THRILLER SERIES
ROGUE FORCE (Book #1)
ROGUE COMMAND (Book #2)
ROGUE TARGET (Book #3)
ROGUE MISSION (Book #4)
ROGUE SHOT (Book #5)

LUKE STONE THRILLER SERIES
ANY MEANS NECESSARY (Book #1)
OATH OF OFFICE (Book #2)
SITUATION ROOM (Book #3)
OPPOSE ANY FOE (Book #4)
PRESIDENT ELECT (Book #5)
OUR SACRED HONOR (Book #6)
HOUSE DIVIDED (Book #7)

FORGING OF LUKE STONE PREQUEL SERIES
PRIMARY TARGET (Book #1)
PRIMARY COMMAND (Book #2)
PRIMARY THREAT (Book #3)
PRIMARY GLORY (Book #4)
PRIMARY VALOR (Book #5)
PRIMARY DUTY (Book #6)

AN AGENT ZERO SPY THRILLER SERIES
AGENT ZERO (Book #1)
TARGET ZERO (Book #2)
HUNTING ZERO (Book #3)
TRAPPING ZERO (Book #4)

FILE ZERO (Book #5)
RECALL ZERO (Book #6)
ASSASSIN ZERO (Book #7)
DECOY ZERO (Book #8)
CHASING ZERO (Book #9)
VENGEANCE ZERO (Book #10)
ZERO ZERO (Book #11)
ABSOLUTE ZERO (Book #12)

PROLOGUE

A private harbor just east of Malaga, on Spain's Mediterranean coast
11 p.m.

Mounir Zerhouni stepped out of his Maserati, took a deep breath of the sea air, and knew he was home. He'd been inland for too long—searching, researching, questioning.

From the Biblioteca Nacional, Spain's vast national library in Madrid, to dusty, old, municipal archives in Santander on the country's northern coast, to little antique shops and antiquarian bookstores scattered throughout the Iberian peninsula, he had searched.

And his search had led him and his men home.

To the Mediterranean. To the sea. To where he belonged.

He savored the moment. Savored the view of the marina that was spread out before him, the yachts and speedboats bobbing slightly in the water, illuminated by a few dim lights whose glow was reflected in the water like shimmering stars. He listened to the cry of gulls overhead, and the thumping of the boats as they gently bumped against the pier. He turned and looked back toward land, where to the west shone the distant lights of the port of Malaga. Between the city and the private marina was a curve of shoreline jutting out into the sea which rose, black in the night, up and up to an illuminated summit where a massive stone fortress stood. Towers and walls held a commanding view of both the port and the smaller cove in which he now stood.

The fort had been built to protect against pirates. To protect against people like him.

From the Middle Ages until the end of the nineteenth century, the Barbary pirates were the terror of the Mediterranean. They raided all along the Portuguese, Spanish, and Italian coasts, hunting for booty and slaves to sell in the markets of Algiers and Tunis and Tangier. The braver captains ventured as far as England and Ireland. One epic voyage went as far as Iceland.

Three other men emerged from the Maserati—a Somali, a Malay, and a Berber like him. His trusted officers. The best from his crew. Hard men quick with a knife and dead shots with a gun, and some of

1

the finest sailors in all the world. In the countless battles they had fought against the ships they had raided, and the other crews that had tried to take their plunder, he had saved each of their lives, and they had saved his.

When Mounir Zerhouni had been a little boy in a village on the slopes of Mount Zerhoun, from which his Berber tribe takes its name, he had been entranced by the tales of the village *hakawati*, the storyteller, tales of the daring pirate captains who struck fear into the hearts of the powerful empires of the Spanish and English.

Mounir had sat there on the cold floor of tamped earth, as the wind howled down from the mountains, and listened to a time when his people had been great.

Now who remembered them? Morocco was ruled by the lowlanders, the descendants of the Arab invaders. The Berber language, Amazigh, had only gotten equal status with Arabic a couple of years ago. And they still did not have any real representation in government. The Arabs ran everything.

And even the name of the pirates had been changed. Barbary, not Berber, so only a few scholars knew the famous pirates had been from his people—a great people who once raided and ruled across North Africa and the Mediterranean.

They would again. He had sworn it.

Mounir turned back toward the sea, back to where his destiny had always taken him.

For there, on that yacht at the far end of the left-hand pier, lay not only his destiny, but the destiny of his entire people.

"Stay here," he told his three officers. "I'll handle this myself."

"Take a gun," the Malay told him. "It could be a trap."

Mounir shook his head. "It isn't. He doesn't know what he has."

"We're here if you need backup," his fellow Berber said.

"I'm not the one who needs backup," Mounir said with a chuckle. "He is."

Mounir strode down the pier, his lean body moving with the strength and grace of a Barbary leopard, the famed predator of the Atlas Mountains. His eyes took in all the details around him—the quality of the boats and what they said about the wealth of their owners, which ones had signs of people sleeping on them and which had been left while their crew slept in town, the locks and burglar alarms that some of them had. Nothing escaped his notice.

The man he sought was paying attention too. On the yacht at the far end of the pier, the spot in the marina with the quickest access to the open sea, a light shone through a curtained porthole. A broad-shouldered man emerged, wearing a thin sweater and a sailor's cap, and moved from the ship to the pier with the rolling, easy gait of an experienced sailor. His bushy, white moustache made a stark contrast to his deeply tanned, seamed face.

"Señor Zerhouni. How good of you to come."

This was said in Spanish, and Mounir replied in kind.

"I'm glad you agreed to see me, Señor Barrado."

"Anyone interested in cartography is always welcome on my boat."

Mounir reached the older man, and they shook hands. Lucas Barrado's hand was calloused, his grip firm.

"Come inside."

They entered. Mounir found himself in the cabin of a well-appointed yacht, not rich, but functional and well cared for. Benches that could turn into bunks stood to either side, with a narrow table in between. A tiny kitchen and pantry took up much of the rest of the space. Through a door, he could see the ship's wheel plus a radio and navigation equipment.

"No crew?" Mounir asked.

"I always sail alone."

Mounir smiled. "Good man."

"Can I offer you coffee or tea? Or would you like something stronger?"

"I'll take whiskey if you have it."

Barrado opened a small cabinet and pulled out a bottle of whiskey and two glasses.

"You live in Spain all your life? Your Spanish is perfect."

"I was born in Andalucía. My parents come from the Atlas and worked here on an agricultural visa, coming up every year to pull in the harvest. My mother was pregnant and gave birth to me on Spanish soil."

Barrado grinned and poured Mounir a generous measure. "Lucky you."

"It's a beautiful language. And I love the food."

"I've sailed all along the Moroccan coast. Some wonderful ports there. Cheers."

3

They clinked glasses and took a sip of their whiskey. Barrado had poured it straight. Didn't even need to ask. A true sailor. Mounir felt the smooth liquid go down his throat to warm his insides.

Barrado put down his glass. "As I told you on the phone, I think you'll be disappointed."

"I'm sure I won't. May I see it?"

Barrado reached into a shelf built under the bench he sat on and pulled out a waterproof case from which he removed a three-ring binder. Placing it on the table, he opened it. Mounir leaned forward, his heart beating fast. Inside, set between two clear sheets of archival, acid-free plastic, was an old parchment map.

The Berber pirate studied it with an expert eye. It was well-drawn, no doubt by a ship's navigator, and the style spoke of the late eighteenth century.

Mounir had become an expert on ancient documents, an expertise he never thought he'd need, an expertise he now knew would bring pride back to his people and unimaginable wealth to himself and his crew.

The map showed the coast of Venezuela, each cove and peninsula drawn with precision. Between one bay and the two islands just to the northeast of it, the cartographer triangulated a point, showing the bearings from each of the nearby landmarks to pinpoint a spot in the Caribbean.

Mounir studied it, a prickling running all over his skin. Yes, this was it. The date was right, the signature "Joaquino" in the lower right-hand corner was right, and while he hadn't known the exact location it pointed to, that looked right too.

Mounir looked up at the old sailor.

"How much do you want for it?" He had to play the part for a little while longer.

"You're a fellow sailor, so I'll level with you. This is a fake. I mean, it's an old fake, so it has curiosity value, but no pirate ship sank there. There's no historical record of that."

No historical record you've found. I dug deeper.

Dug right into the chest of the collector I got my information from.

"I'm still interested. Can you tell me something of its provenance?"

"The original was drawn in 1768 after the *Santo Santiago* disappeared with a load of plunder. There's no record that it sank in the Caribbean, or anywhere else for that matter. My theory is that they sailed off to retire somewhere. Perhaps Brazil, or maybe they even rounded Tierra Del Fuego and went to Chile. This map was one of several copies made in the 1790s and sold to treasure hunters. It might not even be an accurate copy of the original map, not that that matters."

Actually, it is the original, but I'm the only man left alive who knows that.

"I'm still interested. Where did you buy it?"

"From the estate sale of a collector in Gran Canaria."

Mounir nodded. That's what he'd heard.

"I have some other things you might be interested in," the old sailor said and dug into his cabinet. He pulled out several more folders and spread them out. Maps of all the continents and principal waterways of the world, dating from the late seventeenth to early nineteenth centuries.

"That's quite a collection," Mounir said, studying them with admiration.

"I can give you a very good price. I'm afraid I'm not as young as I used to be, and I want to leave something to my grandchildren."

"I want to leave a legacy as well," Mounir said, rising, "and while I'd happily give you top price for the map you think is fake and buy some of these other items, too, I'm afraid I can't let you live."

Lucas Barrado stared at him open-mouthed for a moment, then burst into laughter. "That's a good one. Want another drink?"

Mounir shook his head. "I'm not joking, my friend. I told you this because you are a fellow sailor, and a fellow sailor always deserves a fair fight. Get up."

"Don't you think this joke has gone far enough?" Barrado asked, a note of uncertainty cutting into his voice.

"I'm not joking. Get up."

Barrado studied him a moment longer, then chuckled, looking away and waving his hand in a dismissive gesture.

The old sailor grabbed the bottle of whiskey by the neck, leapt up, and swung it at Mounir's head.

He moved remarkably fast for a man his age, and the arm that swung that heavy bottle was thicker and harder than many an athlete forty years younger, but Mounir was just as strong and far faster.

The Berber grabbed Barrado's wrist and used his own momentum to slam him down on the table. He plucked the whiskey bottle from his hand, taking care not to let any of the liquid draining out to hit the precious old maps, then raised the bottle to strike.

The old man wasn't done fighting yet. He rose up, a marlinspike in his hand. Mounir had to dive back to keep from getting skewered. Barrado must have hidden it under the table just in case the deal turned nasty.

Barrado, glowering, eyes sparking, circled the table and came in for the kill.

Mounir threw the bottle with all his force at the older man's face from barely two paces away.

At that range, Barrado had no time to dodge.

The sailor stumbled back—his face a red ruin—fell and smacked his head against the bulkhead. He slumped to the ground, unconscious or dead.

Mounir strangled him just to make sure.

Once the man was definitely dead, Mounir stood over him for a moment, touching his heart with the palm of his hand to show respect. Then he gathered up the maps and searched the boat for more valuables. Other than a small amount of money and a watch, which he took, he found nothing.

He also took the marine radio, radar, and sonar systems. He wanted it to look like a robbery gone bad, and he didn't want the police to realize what he had truly come here to steal.

With the electronics tucked under his arm, he poked his head out of the cabin and studied the pier. No one in sight. The fight had been brief and not very loud, and he had noticed none of Barrado's neighbors had their lights on as he came in. None of them had their lights on now either.

Mounir got back on the pier and walked quickly to the waiting Maserati.

As he hopped in, the Somali sitting behind the wheel turned on the engine and flashed him a broad grin.

"You get what you came for?"

"Yes, shipmate. We'll be the most famous crew since Blackbeard or the Barbarossa brothers."

"And the richest," the Somali replied.

"There are more things in the world than wealth, my friend," Mounir said, taking a last look at the marina as the car pulled away. "There's power and fame."

"We'll have all three," the Malay said from the back seat.

"We will," Mounir said and nodded. "Very, very soon. And the world will tremble at the mention of our names."

CHAPTER ONE

The Greek coastline, just east of Athens
8:15 a.m.
The next morning

Jacob Snow sped his red Camaro along the seaside road to his bungalow, the needle touching a hundred. He was on his way to a date, at least he hoped so, but his shoulders were tense, and his brow was set in more concentration than the winding highway warranted.

He was on his way to meet his on again/off again girlfriend Gabriella Cremonesi, a gorgeous Italian documentary and wildlife photographer. Ten years younger than Jacob, she was as devoted to her career as he was and wanted nothing more than some fun with no romantic entanglements.

That's what Jacob wanted too. In his line of work, asking for anything long-term from a woman wouldn't be fair. He wasn't sure he'd be alive next week, let alone next year.

And something in her voice when she called had told him danger lurked nearby.

Her voice had been hushed, almost a whisper, and she called far earlier in the morning than usual.

"Could you come down to the Poseidon Taverna? I think someone's been following me."

That had immediately set off alarm bells. Gabriella was on assignment in Athens, filming a refuge for sea birds on a cluster of rocky little islands just off the coast, a lucky assignment that brought the beautiful globetrotter close to home.

Not that he could ever show her his home. The location was top secret.

As he gunned the powerful engine up to 120, he ran through the rest of the conversation.

"Why do you think someone's following you?"

"I went down alone to the beach to catch some second unit shots of the dawn. My crew is busy editing today. I noticed a man walking there. I didn't think much of him until he started approaching. I called

7

to him to keep back because I was going to do a panning shot. He just stopped and stared. Creeped me out. Then a jogger came down the cliff path, and he turned around and went away."

"Did you see him again?"

"Yes. When I went back up the cliff path to get into my car, he was at the scenic overlook. He was facing the sea, but I could see him glancing over his shoulder at me. But that's not all. I went here, to the Poseidon Taverna, to get some breakfast, and just two minutes ago, he stopped at the seaside window and looked in. He looked right at me!"

"Ok. I'll be right there. Stay in the taverna where the waiter can see you."

He took a sharp curve, risking his life by straddling the center line, then cut hard to avoid a truck coming in the other direction. Jacob was so keyed up that he didn't even hear the irate driver's blaring horn. Nor did he see the rugged hills to his right, punctuated by traditional, whitewashed homes with red tile roofs, or the glittering blue Mediterranean to his left, its blue sky puffy with white clouds, and a few distant tankers on the horizon.

All he saw was the road, and all he thought of was the possibilities.

He told himself that it was simply a stalker. Gabriella Cremonesi was a beautiful woman, after all, and she had been alone on that beach with the guy until the jogger showed up. Then he had waited for her at the scenic overview. Jacob knew that beach, and he knew the guy could see her on the beach from there. The perv probably took a few photos while he was at it. Then, when Gabriella drove away, he hopped into his own car and followed.

Now, he was lurking around the taverna.

That was the most likely explanation.

But Jacob Snow hadn't survived a couple dozen missions with the CIA by discounting less likely explanations.

The other explanation, the one he desperately wanted not to be true, was that someone was stalking him through her.

They'd been casually dating for more than a year and had been seen in public many times in Athens and along the lovely stretch of coastline to the east of Greece's capital. He had never brought her anywhere close to his house, but if some spotter for one of the many terrorist groups or security agencies for hostile governments had been watching for a while and discovered a pattern in his movements, they could have narrowed down the location of his house to this general area.

And what better way to get him to come out of hiding than to make a show of stalking her so she would do exactly what she did do—make a frightened call to him and get him to come running?

But he couldn't stay away. If it was a stalker, he couldn't leave Gabriella to deal with him alone. If it was something more sinister and he didn't show, then they might decide to kidnap her.

He had to handle this carefully. The Poseidon Taverna was coming up.

Jacob wished he knew the taverna and its surroundings better. It was a touristy place, a popular stopping point for bus tours thanks to its incredible sea view. Not Gabriella's kind of place at all, but it was the only place open this early for breakfast.

Jacob ran through the tactical situation. The first bus probably hadn't shown up there yet. He usually didn't see any on this road until nine. That meant she was likely alone in the taverna except for the staff and one or two other early risers.

Good. Fewer people meant fewer innocent bystanders, fewer witnesses, and fewer possibilities for who was the bad guy.

But if they had the place staked out, he could get caught in sniper fire as soon as he showed up.

His tires squealed as he braked hard and swung across the lane to stop at one of the road's many scenic overlooks. It wasn't the same overlook Gabriella had mentioned, but one less than a mile from the Poseidon Taverna.

A quick glance around showed no one in sight. A car passed by on the highway, but that was the only sign of life except for the distant ships and the seagulls. Jacob grabbed a sports bag from the passenger's seat. Inside was a compact but powerful set of binoculars, a compact MP5 submachine gun, a couple of spare clips, and two stun grenades taken from his personal arsenal at home.

Slinging it over his shoulder, the zipper open halfway to allow easy access to the death hidden inside, Jacob got out of the car and raced across the two-lane coastal highway. Within moments, he was leaping from rock to rock up the slope like a mountain goat.

Within two minutes, he was on the crest of the ridge. He ran along it, glancing every few steps down on the coastal road below.

The Poseidon Taverna came into view up ahead, a long, rectangular building with a roof of red tiles, a large parking lot facing the road, and a covered patio facing the sea. Gabriella was driving a rental, so Jacob didn't know which of the four cars in the parking lot was hers.

Jacob only looked at the taverna for a moment before cutting to the right to get out of sight of the building and the road.

He sprinted, not wanting to waste time, worried that the stalker or someone worse might make a move.

God, he hoped it was a stalker. He'd beat the crap out of him, Gabriella would be suitably impressed, and they'd spend the rest of the day sightseeing and making love.

If the situation was as he feared, then he had a whole lot of trouble on his hands. Not only would he have to take out a threat on his home turf, but he'd also end up with his cover blown.

First thing first—he needed to flank the taverna, assess the situation, and then neutralize any threat.

It was a hard run under the hot, Greek sun, winding around boulders and olive trees, going up and down the rough terrain atop the ridge, all the while he was going over and over in his mind what dangers his innocent friend could be facing.

He made it, sweating but not out of breath, to a position directly behind the taverna. Jacob lay down and crawled forward, his sports bag slung across his back, the weapons inside pressing against his damp shirt with a reassuring weight.

He got to the edge of the ridge, hid behind a rock outcropping, and scanned the area.

No one was in the parking lot. A couple of cars sped by on the highway. They didn't slow before they passed out of sight. After a minute, a man in a white apron stepped out of the taverna and stood facing the parking lot. He seemed to be doing something with his hands. Jacob was too far away to tell what.

Jacob pulled out the binoculars and focused on him. The guy was smoking. He had no visible weapons, and he wasn't looking around like a sentry would.

The man turned and spoke to someone inside before turning back to face the parking lot, taking another drag of his cigarette.

Jacob scanned the area. He saw no one. The smoker, who Jacob was now 99% sure was the cook, tossed his cigarette away and went back inside, leaving the door open to catch the morning breeze. Or so he could watch the parking lot unseen from the darker interior.

Feeling somewhat reassured and yet still wary, Jacob stood and scrambled down the slope. While this made him clearly visible, regular civilians would assume he was a hiker who had lost his way, while any bad guys would divert their attention away from Gabriella inside the taverna and focus on him. The terrain was rough enough to provide him with plenty of cover if he ended up needing it.

Assuming he saw any gunmen before they took a shot. His gaze roved the nearby slope and building, stumbling twice when he didn't pay enough attention to where he was running.

No shots came. Jacob got all the way down the slope to the side of the highway and saw no one peek around the building or appear at the windows or door. He got no response from anyone in the area except a curious look from a passing trucker.

Feeling somewhat foolish, he darted across the highway to the taverna entrance.

He peered through the open door, his eyes trying to make out the dim interior after being out in the bright sunlight. An older Greek couple sat at a table. A waiter stood with his back to him, looking out through the large windows that opened out onto the patio.

Jacob headed right and peeked through the still-open door the smoker had entered. As he suspected, it was a kitchen. The smoker was busy frying up some eggs while a pimply teenager washed dishes, bobbing to music on his earbuds.

Jacob tiptoed past the open doorway and made his way around the building. He could see the patio, a large rectangle of flagstones bordered with potted plants and a sloping roof above. Several tables were set outside. Only one was occupied.

Gabriella sat alone, occasionally looking over her shoulder back inside.

Was the stalker in there? He hadn't seen him, but there had been a few blind spots.

Jacob hurried back to the front door and adjusted the sports bag to hang by his right side. He put one hand inside and gripped the MP5. Then he strolled into the taverna, his mannerisms casual, his nerves strung, his senses razor sharp.

His eyes scanned the interior. No one but the older couple and the waiter, unless the guy had hidden in the bathroom.

The waiter turned to him.

"Welcome, sir," he said in English. "Would you like to sit inside or outside?"

"Outside, thank you."

Jacob passed by him and out onto the patio. No one but Gabriella.

The young Italian woman turned and saw him.

She rose, giving him a relieved smile. He noticed she had changed her hairstyle.

He smiled, too, equally relieved. There was no stalker in sight, no shots from cover. She was safe.

A moment later, he noticed the unattended bag at the next table.

A simple gym bag. It looked stuffed to capacity. He could see a hard edge pushing out the fabric on one side. It lay directly under one of the tables, half blocked from view by the chairs carefully crowded around it.

"Gabriella, run inside!"

Her face registered confusion. The next instant, there was a blinding flash and an ear-splitting roar. Gabriella was blown to the side, blood spraying from her body from countless wounds. Jacob felt himself get hurled into the air.

He   hit   something   hard   and   knew   no   more.

CHAPTER TWO

A field near Asilah, northwestern Morocco

Jana Peters wiped her hands on her jeans and let out a sigh. She and her crew had backfilled the last trench of her archaeological excavation.

It had been a rewarding three months, during which they discovered a Roman villa complete with a giant, floor mosaic depicting all twelve signs of the zodiac. Her team had worked hard, covering for her during two unexpected absences when she had to "rush off to Europe to help her sick sister."

In fact, she had been saving the world. Twice.

That kind of made it hard to focus on archaeology.

Still, it had been a satisfying dig, and their many discoveries would ensure she'd get funding to come back. Just two more days of finishing up some lab work, then the long flight home and an even longer process of applying for grants and writing up the results of the field season.

Brian Tanner walked up to her. An older graduate student who had a career in a different line of work before switching to archaeology, he was more or less her age, and she was more or less interested.

He was most definitely interested.

"Looks like we're just about done," he said, turning his handsome face to her. His blue eyes looked quite attractive now that his face had developed such a deep tan.

"Yeah, just about," she said, looking into those eyes. They registered interest and hesitancy.

"How's your sister doing?"

"On the mend."

"I'm glad. Hopefully you won't get called away before we pack up," he said with a chuckle.

"You never know," Jana whispered.

She thought of that strange man with whom her life had become bound up. Jacob Snow.

Jana had known of him vaguely from a long time ago, when her father took him under his wing. Dad had spent more time with him than he had with her, training him or running off on some mission or other. She didn't know the details. Couldn't know the details.

But she'd find out more. She had a way now.

All her adult life she had resented her father's absences. As she reached adulthood, she had given him an ultimatum—attend her twenty-first birthday or she'd cut him off. He didn't come, giving some vague excuse that was obviously a coverup for gunning down bad guys in some godforsaken land.

She had hated him for that and had carried that hate as a heavy weight for a long time now.

In the past couple of months, her view had softened. Through a complex series of events, her expertise had been needed twice in missions Jacob had been tasked with. She had seen the other side of the world, the hidden side where powerful forces fought to bring order or chaos to a planet of sleepwalkers.

She had seen just how close the world was to slipping over the brink, and she had helped Jacob pull it back.

This time.

There would be new threats, new evils. She understood that now.

"You're worried about her," Brian said.

"Hmm?" Jana had been so lost in her own thoughts that she had all but forgotten they were in a conversation.

"Your sister."

"Oh. Yes. There's a lot to worry about."

"I wish I could help."

Jana gave a helpless shrug. "So do I."

"Well, I can't help your sister, but maybe I could cheer you up." Brian hesitated, then spoke in a rush. "How about we go to that little seafood place in Asilah? Omar's cooking is great, but I could use a change. Dig food gets repetitive after a while."

Jana looked at him and saw nervousness and expectation written all over his face. She didn't need to be told that the "we" did not include the rest of the crew.

They'd been circling each other all field season. She had been attracted to him, but unsure she wanted to start something when it would end with the excavation. He lived in another state. She sensed that he hesitated for the same reasons, plus the fact that she was technically his boss.

14

Then Jacob had shown up and thrown even more emotion into the mix, emotions she didn't want to even put a name to let alone work out consciously.

"Sure. Let's go," she said. His face lit up. Then she remembered the appointment she had for a Zoom call to a former colleague of her dad. "I need to be back by ten, though. I have a call with … family."

Brian gave her an uncertain smile. "No problem."

***

At five minutes to ten, Jana sat in her tent, staring at her laptop. She had a satellite uplink to make the Zoom call and wore earbuds so none of the crew passing by her tent could hear Hank Gunner's side of the conversation. She'd keep her questions nonincriminating. She had already heard the crew whispering about her two absences and the attempt on her life. Not everyone believed the sick sister story, although they had no clue about the real truth.

Poor Brian. That dinner had not been what he had hoped for. The food was delicious, the view over the Atlantic at sunset was stunning, but she had not been the best company. She couldn't help but obsess over what Gunner might tell her in this call, and that made her distant and unresponsive.

She hoped he didn't take that as rejection because it wasn't.

At least she wasn't quite sure if it was or not.

But enough. She had questions she wanted answers to, and Hank Gunner was the man to ask.

She licked her lips, checked the clock for the fifth time, and hit dial.

It rang. Jana shifted in her seat. Gunner was one of the many men who told her at her father's memorial service (there had been no body) that she could call him anytime, for anything. She knew he and the others meant it, and yet she had never reached out. She didn't want to be reminded of a relationship that had withered and opportunities that had been missed.

Gunner picked up on the third ring. His craggy face appeared in the frame.

Jana blinked with surprise. His salt and pepper hair had gone full gray, and the lines she had remembered in his face had deepened. Bags had formed under his eyes.

How long had it been? Gunner was older than her father, but at the memorial service, he had been in rugged middle age. Now aging had caught up with him.

The face may have been old, but the smile was warm. "Hey, Jana! Look at you hunkered down in a tent in Morocco. How did the excavation go? I saw that mosaic on CNN. Great stuff!"

"Yeah, we made quite a find. We've excavated a large portion of the villa. I'm going to apply for funding to come back next year and do the rest, as well as search for the outbuildings and nearby peasants' settlement to put the villa in its proper context."

"If it's federal funding you're after, or something from the UN, I can put in a few calls."

"No. I can get all that myself."

Gunner nodded and smiled like a proud uncle. "Standing alone, just like your dad taught you." There was a pause. Both stared at each other. The old CIA operative went on in a softer voice. "It's about him, isn't it?"

"Yes."

"I'll tell you anything I'm allowed to tell you."

She could see the discomfort in his eyes, the struggle between his desire to tell her everything and his sense of duty, his oath, not to.

"Actually, I need to get in contact with someone who knows more about the questions I specifically need to ask. Jacob Snow."

"There are limits to what he can tell you too."

"I know."

"When did you see him last?"

"A few weeks ago."

Gunner blinked with surprise. "Really?"

"I've been called in as a … civilian consultant I guess you would call it, twice now to work with Jacob. The missions were such a whirlwind I never got a chance to sit down and have a proper talk with him."

"Wait. You were on Jacob's last two missions?"

"Yeah. You know about them?"

"Not much. Enough. Thank you for your service."

Gunner had just paid her the best compliment he knew how to give. Jana felt a warm feeling expand from her heart.

Oh God, I'm falling into this. I don't want to end up with Dad's mindset.

"Thank you, that means a lot," she replied with more emotion than she wanted to reveal. She lowered her eyes. "It was … difficult."

"You had to leave your excavation. You had to leave your responsibility and what you loved in order to fight for the greater good."

Resentment bubbled up inside her. She wanted to shout at him that directing an archaeological excavation was nothing compared to raising a child, but she couldn't speak. Gunner had kids of his own. Kids he probably didn't see enough of when they were young.

Did they resent him like she resented Dad?

"Yeah, well, it was tough." *I had to kill people. Bad people. Evil people. But still people.* She cleared her throat. "Jacob said he'd get in touch sometime. I don't think he will. I was wondering if there was any way I could get in touch with him. Do you know where he lives?"

"Somewhere in Europe, although he travels even more than you do. I don't know the address. I don't even know the country. And I couldn't give it to you if I did."

Jana slumped. "Oh."

"He has a public phone number that he gives to friends and acquaintances who don't know what he really is. It changes from time to time, and I don't have the current one. I can get it, though. Give me a day or two."

"That would be great. Thanks."

For a long moment, neither said anything. Jana summoned up the courage to speak.

"So, what do you know about Jacob and my father?"

"What do you know already?"

"Dad taught him some things, I know that. Spent time with him. Jacob was very vague, and Dad hardly spoke of him at all. It was annoying. Jacob got to spend more time with Dad than I did, and neither of them talked about it. Like it was some big secret."

"Well, I suppose you know why they had to keep it secret now."

Jana shook her head. "I don't want to know about the missions. I want to know about them. They seemed more than just comrades-in-arms. I have his old pictures, and they went to ball games together, did cookouts, went hunting."

Jana could feel the jealousy rising in her heart and hear it coming out in her words.

"It takes a lot more than training to save a man," Hank Gunner said. "It takes mentorship."

"Save a man?"

The older operative's face turned grim. "Jacob was serving in a different capacity."

"Under another name," Jana cut in, remembering that American soldier they had bumped into who had called out to him in Jerusalem, calling him Mitch.

"I can't talk about that. What I can tell you is that Jacob was serving his country when there was an episode."

"An episode?"

"I can't tell you exactly what—"

"Of course you can't," she grumbled.

"I'm trying here, Jana."

"Sorry. Go on."

"Jacob had to stop something bad from happening. Really bad. But it meant going against his own people. And that broke him."

"He had to take out a double agent?"

"Something like that. Not really. Let's just say the good guys turned out to be the bad guys. He did what he had to do but that tipped him over the edge. He was … in a dark place for a time. Aaron pulled him out of it. Your father saved him."

"Jacob had a breakdown?" Suddenly, she didn't feel so angry with him anymore.

"Far, far worse than a breakdown, Jana."

"Is he all right now?" The depth of her concern surprised her.

"No one in this business is all right. He's stable, if that's what you're asking, and I'm sure he feels a deep sense of loyalty to you because you're Aaron's daughter."

"So, Dad pulled him out of his breakdown, or whatever you want to call it?"

"He saved his soul, Jana. And yes, that meant a lot of time with him, time away from you. All those ball games and barbeques were part of the healing process. And the training he gave him when he brought Jacob into the CIA, well, that was classified. You couldn't join in that."

"But the socializing. We could have done that together."

Hank Gunner shook his head. "Your father needed to keep you safe."

"Keep me safe? Are you saying Jacob is dangerous?"

"Not now. Not to you. But back then …" Gunner raised his hand and waved it in the air.

"Just how bad was this breakdown?"

"Bad enough that Aaron was right to keep you away from him until he was stable. And after that he was on missions and needed to keep away from you for security reasons. I'm sorry Aaron had to spend so much time away, but he was saving lives. It's a hard thing to balance. Trust me, I know. But he did what he thought was right. Did he get it right all the time? No. None of us do. But he loved you, and he loved Jacob, and he did what he could for you both. And that's all I can tell you. I'll get you that number in a day or two. Call him. I can't guarantee he'll answer. But it's the best I can do."

"All right. Thanks. You take care, Hank."

"God bless."

Jana ended the call with more question than answers.

She did know one thing, though. She was going to get in touch with Jacob, and she was going to learn a whole lot more.

She'd make him talk.

CHAPTER THREE

One week later ...

Jacob lay in bed at home, feeling more pain on the inside than from his fifteen stitches, fractured wrist, large patches of second-degree burns, and a healing concussion.

Gabriella was dead. Beautiful, talented, warm, and far too young Gabriella Cremonesi.

An innocent victim. Collateral damage in the war between good and evil.

Who did it? A crack team of CIA investigators gathered from all over the European Bureau were investigating and had come up with nothing. No one had claimed any responsibility, chatter hadn't revealed any known terrorists or enemy operatives in the area, and the physical evidence was scanty.

Whoever did this had planned very, very well.

The team would continue its investigation until they found out who did it and make them pay.

The bomb had been a simple but powerful model, within the abilities of most terrorist cells or large criminal groups. It had killed Gabriella instantly, thrown Jacob against the back wall of the taverna, and the shockwave had passed through the open windows to knock down everyone inside. Luckily, no one else was killed, although that old couple were in serious but stable condition in the local hospital.

Jacob lay in bed with earbuds on, scanning through Dark Web chatter. He'd been stuck on light duty since he had been released from the U.S. military hospital in Crete. He'd wanted to join the hunt and got warned off by his boss, station director Tyler Wallace. When he showed up at the war room anyway, Wallace had told him he'd be relieved from duty if he didn't back off.

"You need rest," Wallace had said. "You need to work through this."

"The way I work through things is to work," Jacob had snapped at him. "You think I won't be objective in hunting for the bombers? Well, you're right. But I need to be hunting someone. If you don't give me some work, I'll tape hundred-dollar bills all over my body, walk through the port at night, and rip the throat out of the first guy who tried to rob me."

"Fine. You can monitor communications. But you can take a break anytime you feel like it."

"Monitoring communications? That's for noobs."

"It's that or monitored rest in Malta."

"When do I start?"

Tyler Wallace wasn't the kind of man you defied twice.

So, Jacob lay in his bed, a laptop resting on his lap as he scrolled through intercepted conversations, trying to find something worth the CIA's limited resources. Being fluent in several different languages, they'd given him a wide spectrum of communication lines.

Right now, he was listening in on a supposedly encrypted chat between a wholesaler in Libya and a retailer in Sicily. At least that's what they called themselves. Just what they were trading in wasn't clear, except they were using a speedboat to cross the Mediterranean to get to Sicily.

Considering that it the origin point was Libya, it probably wasn't drugs. Europe's hash mostly came from Morocco and its designer drugs from Israel. Libya mostly dealt in illegal migrants, trafficked women, and the occasional terrorist trying to infiltrate the European Union.

He sincerely hoped it was a terrorist. Then he could conveniently forget to inform Tyler Wallace, go to the delivery point, and gun everyone down. That would make him feel better.

Except that it wouldn't. The pain and guilt of having his girlfriend die for no other crime than knowing him would stay with him for a long, long time.

He shoved those feelings deep down and got back to work.

"They'll be coming day after tomorrow to the usual place," the Libyan said.

"How many?"

"Twenty-eight jeans and eight scarves."

"Any small sizes?"

"Two of each."

Jacob immediately lost interest. "Jeans" and "scarves" were standard human smuggler slang for "men" and "women." "Small sizes" meant children. This was a shipment of illegal immigrants, desperate individuals paying smugglers to put them in an undersized motorboat and send them across the hazardous Mediterranean. He made a note about the details of the conversation for the CIA to forward to the Italian Coast Guard and moved to another channel.

This one was a private chatroom on a bulletin board for programming in Pascal. Except that it wasn't. They'd scraped chat threads off an older and since deleted bulletin board and changed the dates to make it look like a live community. The real action happened in the private chatrooms. The CIA had hacked it years ago, and it had delivered up some pretty good results.

He found two chatrooms currently in operation. The first turned out to involve the sale of a small shipment of MDMA. Boring. He switched to the second one.

They were speaking in Spanish, one of the languages Jacob spoke since it was commonly used Morocco, one of his main areas of operation. The first speaker was a native Castilian, with the lisping accent so common in that dialect. The second speaker spoke almost the same way, except with a slightly more blunted accent he could not quite place. It wasn't regional Spanish. Perhaps a fluent foreigner?

Speaker One: "Did you get it?"

Speaker Two: "Yes."

Speaker One: "You sure it's the right one?"

Speaker Two: "Yeah, yeah. The one Vasquez had in Madrid was the fake, not the one down here."

Speaker One: "I don't know how you can tell those bits of paper apart. They all look the same to me."

Speaker Two (laughs): "It's called studying, shipmate. All you ever study is guns and navigation."

Speaker One (laughs): "And women. You forgot women."

Speaker Two: "Once the map leads us to the treasure, you'll have all the women you want."

Speaker One (quietly): "All the ones still alive. You sure it will still be viable after all this time?"

Speaker Two: "It will. Have faith, shipmate."

Speaker One: "This map. It's clear enough to show us the stuff from the *Nueva Esperanza*?"

Speaker Two: "As clear as you can expect for the era. We'll have to dive for a bit, but the water's pretty shallow there. I checked the charts. If we give it some time, we shouldn't have a problem."

Speaker One: "All right. The vengeance is ready. We'll meet you at the rendezvous."

Speaker Two: "Full up on provisions?"

Speaker One: "Full up. We made sure of that before granting shore leave."

Speaker Two: "Did you arrange the coyote?"

Speaker One: "F's contact worked out."

Speaker Two: "Do you trust this coyote?"

Speaker One: "I trust his greed."

Speaker Two (laughs): "Good enough."

Speaker One: "He'll take us all the way up to tourist central."

Speaker Two: "I can always count on you, shipmate."

Speaker One: "Damn right you can. You're the best leader I've seen since Ibn Bustam in Malacca."

Speaker Two: "He was a hell raiser, but we're going to raise a whole lot more hell than he ever did. See you soon, once I get everything sorted out."

Speaker One: "We'll be waiting."

They hung up. The monitoring system the CIA used automatically recorded everything the operative listened to, and so Jacob moved the file into a folder labeled "Further Investigation."

Something about this one piqued his interest. The mention of treasure got the little boy in him all excited, dreaming of pirates and piles of gold doubloons. A more serious side to his nature thought that possibility wasn't all that silly. They had talked of a ship and navigation, and the first speaker had mentioned someone named Ibn Bustam in Malacca. The Strait of Malacca was a long, narrow stretch of water between the Malay Peninsula and Sumatra and was rife with piracy until a few years ago when a concerted effort by the Malaysian, Indonesian, and Australian navies put the smack down.

A search in the CIA database did not reveal any Ibn Bustam, but that didn't surprise him. Bustam meant "stock market" in Arabic, so his name translated to "son of the stock market." Obviously, a nickname bragging about his business success.

The second speaker, the one with the accent he couldn't quite place, sounded like the leader. He had been going around Spain and perhaps other countries looking for a map. In Madrid, he found a fake, then found the real one "down here." Did that mean somewhere south of Madrid? The Spanish capital was in the dead center of the country so that didn't exactly narrow it down.

He had met someone named Vasquez and then the owner of the real map "down here."

The CIA had access to the criminal databases of most friendly nations, and so Jacob got onto the Spanish national criminal database and searched for someone with the last name Vasquez.

He came up as a murder victim from ten days ago.

Suddenly, Jacob was taking this whole thing a lot more seriously.

Jacob delved into the investigation. Antonio Vasquez was a sixty-two-year-old dealer in antique maps and old books on nautical themes. No criminal record. He had a small shop off Calle Serrano, in the heart of Madrid's upper-class district. His body had been found by his cleaning lady, who had let herself in in the morning and found him stabbed in his back office. Time of death was estimated to have been around ten the previous evening. No signs of a break-in.

The speaker had probably posed as a buyer. Numerous items were missing, including several maps of high value. Prints and hairs of several individuals were retrieved at the scene. No known suspects and no CCTV footage.

Jacob switched over to the list of murders, looking for anyone else who had been murdered in the past two weeks. Luckily, it was a short list. Europe has a far lower murder rate than the United States. Spain had only 298 murders in the entire country in the previous year. By comparison, Chicago had more than 800.

In the past two weeks, other than Vasquez, there had been three murders in the whole of Spain.

One was a woman battered to death by her abusive husband. Another was a member of an Ecuadorian gang hacked to death by a rival gang with machetes. How charming. The third was a yacht owner, killed a week before on his boat in a private marina near Malaga, on Spain's southeastern coast.

Lucas Barrado was a man of private means who spent most of his time sailing the world and was also a known collector of maritime maps. Several items known to be in his possession had been stolen, as well as all the moveable electronics from the yacht.

Spanish police had already made a connection between the two murders and suspected the theft of the electronics was merely to cover up the killer's real motive—the maps.

Jacob agreed.

So, a group of modern-day pirates (assuming Jacob's inner twelve-year-old wasn't letting his imagination run away with him) killed two men in Spain to get some maps, more likely one specific map, taking the others as a coverup. All this to search for some treasure.

A treasure map? Those things still existed in the twenty-first century? Had they ever really existed?

Fascinating stuff, but not really something for the CIA to investigate.

Except for one offhand comment by one of the speakers, the one who sounded like the ship's navigator. When his captain or superior officer had said the navigator would have all the women he wanted, he had replied in a quiet voice,

"All the ones still alive. You sure it will still be viable after all this time?"

Why was he thinking there would be a lot of deaths? And what did he mean by the treasure remaining viable?

Until a couple of months ago, he would have dismissed that as idle chatter, but after finding naturally refined uranium in an ancient Egyptian Canopic jar, he had come to believe that anything was possible.

He sent a request for tracking for the two people in the conversation, and a request that this conversation be forwarded to the Spanish police.

Jacob put his laptop to the side, rubbed his eyes, and did what he knew he shouldn't do—he picked up his public cell phone.

He'd gotten into the habit of scrolling through Gabriella's texts and photos. She'd sent him plenty. Shots of her work, the beautiful birds and animals and landscapes that had been her stock and trade. The cute emojis and notes she'd sent on an almost daily basis.

Jacob grimaced. Most of those he hadn't replied to. An advanced AI system had. It was part of the cover of all senior operatives to have an AI on their public phone, so it never looked like they had any long absences from communication—that they were regular civilians like everyone else.

All those happy moments, chatting with a machine.

The worst of it all was that he hadn't loved her. She'd been a bit of fun, relaxation from a grinding double life.

Had she loved him? She never said so. She sent hearts with a lot of those emojis, but she sent them to her eight-year-old niece too.

Jacob paused, staring at the phone he hadn't yet turned on. He really shouldn't do this.

He did it anyway.

And blinked.

Three calls from Jana. He had put her number into his phone just in case, although he hadn't intended on calling her.

How the hell had she gotten this number?

The AI had ignored the first call from two days ago until the second call came six hours later, then sent a text saying he was busy with work and would get right back to her.

Jana had obviously not bought that and called again early the following morning. The AI had then sent a voice message, using a computer-generated imitation of his own voice only the most sophisticated analysis could have determined wasn't the real thing, to say apologetically that he was too overloaded with work at his NGO to return the call, and that he was flying to Nairobi that afternoon.

Jacob winced. She might not have access to advanced voice recognition software, but she would sure know that was a load of bull.

He stared at the phone a moment longer, wondering what he should do.

And then the question of what he should do got drowned in a tidal wave of emotions that told him what he wanted to do.

He returned the call.

CHAPTER FOUR

"Hello, Jana?"

Jana sat up in her hotel room bed in Rome. Jacob's voice sounded uncertain, hurt. Jana's heart shifted as she heard it. Something was wrong.

"Yeah, it's me. How are you?"

"Um, fine. How did you get this number?"

"An old friend of my dad's."

Long pause.

"Look, Jana. This isn't really a good time."

"What's wrong?"

"Nothing. Work stuff."

"I need to see you."

Another long pause. "I … um … why?"

All of Jana's questions and all of her anger faded as she heard the hurt and confusion in his every syllable. This didn't sound like his voice message at all.

Although she had a sneaking suspicion that was some prerecorded program. Jacob knew she wouldn't have fallen for that story about working for an NGO in Nairobi and thus wouldn't have used it.

"I had some questions. Where are you?" Jana asked.

"Look, Jana, I'm working and—"

"No, you're not. If you were on a …" Jana stopped herself from saying 'mission.' This was probably not a secure line. "… a job then you wouldn't have answered at all. Something's wrong. Maybe I can help."

Jacob whispered something she didn't catch. It sounded like "You can't help."

"Let me come to you. I'm in Rome. Are you close by?"

"I don't really want to deal with questions right now, Jana."

Jana thought for a moment. "Then I won't ask any. I promise. Sounds like you could use some company."

"Yeah," Jacob said with a sigh. "Yeah, I could use that."

"So, let me come to you."

There was another pause, longer this time. Jana could hear sounds on the other end of the line. Crying? Him talking to himself? She wasn't sure.

A little groan. "All right. I'm in Athens."

"I'll be on the next plane. I'll send you the flight details and—"

"Don't do that!" he shouted, and Jana's heart skipped a beat. "Call me when you get into the airport. I'll pick you up."

Now she as sure something was wrong.

And Jacob wanted her there to help deal with it.

She found a last-minute flight leaving for Athens in three hours. It was fully booked except for first class. The price was extortionate, but she paid it.

***

Jana didn't know what she expected when she got out of the terminal at the Athens airport, but she did not expect to be greeted by a stiffly moving, slouched, haunted-eyed man who looked like but did not act like Jacob Snow. His right wrist was wrapped in brown kinesiology tape, and for some reason, he wore a scarf bunched up around his neck despite the warm night.

Jana rushed up to him and lightly touched him on the shoulders. "Jesus, what happened?"

"I can't talk about it," he mumbled, not meeting her eye. "The car's over here."

He took her bag, wincing as he hefted the heavy suitcase, and led her through the parking lot to a red Camaro. Jana almost joked that she expected him to have a car like that, but she bit her tongue.

They got in and drove out of the parking lot.

"I can't take you to my house. The location's classified. I know a good hotel downtown with a view of the Acropolis. It's in the old quarter, almost at the base. You'll like it."

"Great. Thanks. First let's go to some quiet place and I'll buy you a drink."

Jacob let out a little shrug. "All right."

***

A few minutes later, they sat in the corner of a taverna on a back street. A few Greek couples took up the other seats, and two younger,

Greek guys stood at the bar, arguing about the soccer match on television.

The noise they made gave Jacob and Jana cover for their conversation.

"So, tell me what happened," Jana said, leaning forward and putting her hand on his.

"I can't."

"Classified?"

"Yeah."

"Jacob, I've heard so much classified stuff already. Hell, half my field season ended up classified."

Faint smile. No true mirth behind it. And he still wasn't meeting her eye. "Someone tried to kill me."

She had seen that happen a dozen times. Jacob usually cracked jokes about it.

"What was different about this time?"

He took a long pull on his beer, put it down with a smack, and said, "A friend got killed. A civilian."

"Oh, Jacob, I'm so sorry."

To her shock, she saw tears welling in his eyes.

"She didn't know what I do for a living. She was working close by and got spooked because she saw someone following her. That was a trick. Whoever was trying to get me knew about her and knew she would call me. So, I came running to stop what I thought was a stalker. I had my suspicions, scouted out the area, but these guys were good. Very good. I never saw a damn thing. And when I went to meet with her … they set off a bomb."

For a moment neither spoke. Jana kept her hand on his.

"Do you know who did it?"

Jacob shook his head. "It could have been a lot of people. The Company is investigating, but they don't have much to go on. No chatter. No threats. No claim of responsibility. No real evidence."

"Are you badly hurt?"

"Got banged up some. This scarf I'm wearing is to cover some burns. Got them on my chest too. Took some shrapnel in the chest too. Nothing major."

On the outside.

Jana and Jacob sat quietly for a minute, sipping their beers. She felt at a loss. What can you tell someone in this situation? Jacob must have felt consumed by guilt. But telling him it wasn't his fault wouldn't make him feel better. He wouldn't believe it, because if he hadn't been in the CIA, this wouldn't have happened.

"Is there anything I can do to help find these people?"

As soon as she said it, she realized how ridiculous it sounded. She had no idea how to track a terrorist. Still, she had been on two successful missions …

Jacob gave a helpless little shrug, so unlike him.

"No. I'm not even able to help. They won't let me join in the investigation. They think I won't be objective. They got me a bullshit detail monitoring chatter."

"Still a useful task," Jana said, repeating something her father had once said. "It lays the groundwork for most operations."

Jacob snorted. "It's for noobs and people slated for retirement."

"And people who need to heal," Jana said softly. After a moment, she asked, "Find anything interesting?"

If anything could cheer him up, it was work. They were a lot alike in that respect.

"Nothing big, at least no terrorist stuff that I can figure. I did come across one weird conversation, though, coming out of Spain."

"*¿Hablas español?*" Jana asked.

"*Si.*"

They continued in Spanish. If Jacob was going to tell her something juicy, it would be better to speak in a language the other people in the bar were unlikely to understand.

"I was monitoring a private chat room on the Dark Web," Jacob said.

"I've never been on the Dark Web."

"Don't. There's stuff on there you can't unsee. Anyway, these guys sounded like modern-day pirates. There are a lot of them, you know, especially off the Horn of Africa and in the straits around Southeast Asia. One guy seemed to be in charge, talking to his navigator. I think the ship's name is the *Vengeance*. The guy in charge was hunting for a treasure map. He killed a collector in Madrid and then another near Malaga. I found the victims in the Spanish police database. So, these guys want to find the wreck of some ship called the *New Hope*."

"*La Nueva Esperanza,*" Jana murmured. "I've heard of it."

"So, it was some Spanish galleon that got sunk? There are a lot of those out there that people are still looking for. They hauled gold from the New World back to Spain and got sunk by storms or enemy ships. I used to read about them when I was a kid. I don't remember reading about La Nueva Esperanza, though."

"That's because it wasn't a galleon. It wasn't even a warship. It was a colony vessel."

"A colony vessel?"

"Yeah. It was sunk by pirates in 1780 or so. I'd have to look it up. What I do remember is that a famous, early Spanish physician named Sebastián de Ulloa died on board. He was credited with isolating the first virus."

Jacob perked up. "Wait. There was something in the chatter about that. The navigator asked his boss if something could still be viable after all these years and worried about a lot of people dying."

Jana nodded. "From what I remember, there had been an outbreak of what they called 'Black Fever' in what is now Venezuela. It spread like wildfire. Thousands died. Sebastián de Ulloa was a leading physician and researcher at the time, and he risked his life going to the colony to study it. He isolated the virus from patient samples and stored it somehow. Then he intended on sailing back to Spain on a colony ship that had dropped off more migrants and planned to return to Europe. They got attacked by pirates and sunk."

"What happened to the sample?"

"There's no mention as far as I know. But it's not exactly my specialty. I'm an archaeologist of the Roman period. I just know a few things about maritime archaeology because of a, um, colleague I knew a few years back."

Pierre Gaston. More of a treasure hunter than a maritime archaeologist, although he knew his subject as good as any academic. For some reason, Jana decided to skip the fact that they had enjoyed a brief but torrid and exquisitely satisfying love affair. It didn't seem appropriate to the conversation.

Jacob thought for a moment, staring off into space, his beer forgotten. Jana watched him, amazed. That dead look in his eyes had vanished, and the alert spark had returned. He still looked beat, still looked depressed, but he was no longer broken.

All he needed was a few kind words and someone with the insight to get him back on track. Does he really have no one in his life like that?

Or maybe this woman had been that. No, probably not. Jacob had mentioned she didn't know about his double life, and if she didn't know that, then she didn't know the real Jacob Snow.

And yet Jana couldn't help but feel a nagging sense of jealousy about this unnamed woman. She had been someone special to him, that was obvious.

She rejected that thought as base petty. Jacob's friend had been an innocent bystander caught in the crossfire. Whoever she was, she should be mourned, and she should be avenged.

If Jana could help him in that regard, she would.

Jacob snapped his fingers. "There must be a chance it's still viable. They know something we don't, something about how this physician, what's his name?"

"Sebastián de Ulloa."

"Right. How he preserved the sample to make them think they could retrieve it. They want to use it as a bioweapon, or sell it as one, or threaten to use it. That would explain why the navigator worried about a lot of people dying, and why his superior officer thought they could become richer than they ever imagined."

"It seems unlikely."

"Enriched uranium in an ancient Egyptian Canopic jar seems unlikely, but The Sword of the Righteous made a crude nuclear device from it. After that, I stopped being surprised by anything."

"Inform your Caribbean branch. They can investigate."

Jacob shook his head. "The CIA needs something way more solid than what we have here. We need to do this ourselves."

Jana was taken aback. "Ourselves?"

"You want a gang of modern-day Blackbeards running around with a bioweapon?"

"No, but I thought you were stuck on desk duty."

"Wallace said I could take a vacation whenever I wanted. Fine, I'll take a vacation."

"A vacation hunting pirates?"

Jacob grinned, a bit of the old humor coming back to him. "What better vacation can you think of?"

"And you want me to come along?" Jana still couldn't believe her ears.

"You're good at digging up history, and you've already shown me you know more about this period than I do. Let's go to Spain."

Jana suddenly remembered how angry at him she'd been. She crossed her arms and cocked an eyebrow.

"Did it ever occur to you that I might have academic obligations back home?"

"And those are more important than saving the world?" Jacob asked, then cocked an eyebrow, mocking her own expression. "Again?"

Jana rolled her eyes. "Oh, all right."

All right, Jacob Snow. I'll come along on your mission if it makes you feel better about what happened to your friend. But this isn't for free. I'm getting paid this time.

And my payment is some answers.

CHAPTER FIVE

Hunting in the mountains near the Khyber Pass was an ancient sport, and a dangerous one. The range of bare, rugged mountains between Afghanistan and Pakistan, seared by the sun during the day and scoured by bitterly cold winds at night, could only be home to the toughest of animals. The ibex, fast climbers, are prized for their gamey meat and swirled horns, assuming chasing one across the landscape doesn't make the hunter fall into a hidden ravine or snap his ankles on a loose stone.

The rare Himalayan brown bear, which can rip a man's throat out with a single swipe of its powerful paw, are hunted for its warm pelt and rich meat. The liver is especially sought after, a savory meal rich in vitamins in this undernourished region.

Most sought after of all is the all-but-extinct snow leopard. Its soft, pure pelt is such a rarity that it fetches top prices to dealers selling it on to millionaire collectors in Japan and China. A hunter who bags a snow leopard will earn enough to buy a sturdy house, a brand-new AK-47, and some grazing land for his family, assuming he doesn't get torn to shreds first.

But the most ancient game, and the most dangerous, is man. The tough tribes of the Khyber Pass have been fighting blood feuds and personal vendettas for as long as anyone can remember. Every boy yearns to be a great warrior, and they are trained not with the PlayStation, but with the .45 pistol and the Kalashnikov assault rifle. As soon as they are old enough to withstand the recoil, their father and uncles train them how to hunt and shoot, and before they can grow even the first wisps of the beard that all men wear—because the Prophet wore a beard, and no man can call himself a man without one—many youths have already fired at an enemy and been fired upon.

To die in battle is the greatest honor. To kill in battle is the greatest boast.

The best hunter of men in the Khyber Pass was not from a local tribe. He was not Afridi or Shinwari, or a Nuristani trying to retake his ancestral lands from the two Pastun groups that had kicked them out many wars ago. Nor was he an interloper like the Uzbeks or Pakistanis.

He was a foreigner, a lowlander who was not a citizen of Afghanistan or Pakistan.

Even worse, he was an unbeliever.

Or so people whispered.

The fact was, few people ever saw him up close, and those who did died very quickly.

Surely, he must have some help. Some faction of some tribe must give him food and shelter. Whether they did this for money or, strange as it may seem, because they wished to bring peace upon the land, no one could say for sure.

Because the greatest killer of the Khyber Pass was not indiscriminate in his killing. He only went after the radicals. ISIS, Al-Qaeda, The Sword of the Righteous, Ansar el Islam, any group that wanted to wage global jihad found itself targeted by this mysterious killer with the blue eyes and white face.

Except at this moment. Right now, he hunted different game.

Because that game hunted him.

Running down a steep, rocky slope, his boots sending small stones skittering before him, Operative 313 was trying to make himself a target. He knew he was too far away from the man who hunted him for the guy to take a clear shot. The sun, harsh at this altitude, shone from a low angle onto the ridge above, and the man who watched him would not want to risk it glinting off the lens of his scope. He would not want to risk being spotted.

No. The man who hunted Operative 313 was a professional. That much was obvious.

Operative 313 had only spotted him twice in the past two days. Once in the far distance along a glacial scree at twilight, so far that the man with the blue eyes did not realize he was following him. The second time was when Operative 313 crossed over a ridge, one of those knife edges of rock with near-vertical cliff faces on either side that divide so many of the valleys here. Operative 313 had clambered up the west face in a remote portion of the valley just as the morning sun was turning the ridge into a silhouette, casting him in deep shadow. As he got to the summit and edged between two jutting rocks the size of city buses with barely room in between for a man to get through sideways if he took off his pack, he had glanced behind him.

There, on the far end of the valley, he had seen movement.

Only for a second, and from a distance of more than a mile, but that had been enough.

At the far end of the valley, where boulders lay strewn after eroding down from the heights of the next ridge, a shadow flit from one boulder to the next. Operative 313 got the impression of a lean man in local garb, a weapon strapped to his back.

Operative 313 stayed still in the shadowed shelter of the crevasse, waiting for the man to reappear.

He did not.

That told him two things. First, that he had gone prone and was worming his way through the rough terrain where there was enough cover to remain out of sight.

Second, it told him that the man was following him.

It paid to be careful in this area of the world, but if the man was simply trying to cross the valley like he was or cut down it toward a Taliban-ruled village that lay out of sight several miles away, he would have appeared by now.

So, the man was watching, waiting for Operative 313 to descend the other side of the ridge in order to pursue him further.

That left the greatest hunter of men in the Khyber Pass three options—he could take him out with his sniper's rifle, he could lay a trap for him, or he could try to shake him.

The first option was the easiest and the worst.

This was a sensitive area, in the midst of a war between the Taliban, who claimed this valley and the two flanking it, and a local Al-Qaeda commander who had been trying to extract taxes from the villages there. Gunshots would attract attention, and Operative 313 did not want attention.

He'd try the second option first. A trap. To run was not in his nature. Besides, something told him he could not outrun this fellow.

So, he worked his way through the crevasse and began to descend the east face of the ridge as fast as the terrain allowed. He had intended on camping in the crevasse until high noon, because with the sun shining on the eastern cliff, he was far too visible, but now he had to risk the chance of being spotted by a hostile he didn't see in order to shake the hostile he had seen.

He cut to the left, where an easier slope was littered with tumbled stones the size of 1960s Chevys. Like his pursuer, he darted between these, occasionally going prone. The man following him couldn't possibly have made it through up the cliff and through the crevasse yet, but with the sun still low, Operative 313 couldn't spot anyone hiding in the shadows of the far side of the valley. Al-Qaeda had recently gotten a shipment of Pakistani-made snipers rifles, and he didn't want to become target practice.

He got to the bottom of the slope where it leveled out to a rocky valley floor with a narrow river splashing between the stones. Day-old goat droppings told him a herd had passed through here. Footprints interspersed with them showed a man and a boy, no doubt both armed.

Only two people. That meant the rest weren't far. A lone man and boy wouldn't stray too far from their tribal camp of nomads. There was no village within a day's march from this spot. The soil was too rocky for much of the length of the valley to sustain even the meagre cultivation common hereabouts.

Operative 313 found a spot between two of these and went prone. He took a long, steady look around and saw no movement. Then he pulled a rifle case out of his pack. His normal weapon was the Russian-made AK-47 that rarely left his hands. It helped him blend in, but this shot required something a little more specialized.

He opened the case to reveal the parts of a stripped MK 15 Mod 0 SASR (special applications sniper rifle). Its five-round magazine held the hefty .50 BMG ammo, which could punch a hole in the side of an armored personnel carrier at 1,000 meters. Even as the round reached its maximum range of 1,600 meters, it still had the power to perforate a Kevlar vest and ruin the day of whomever wore it.

It was the favored long-range rifle of the Navy Seals. Operative 313 had a lot of respect for the Navy Seals. They had beaten him up once in a bar fight in his younger and stupider days. It had taken three of them to do it, and one ended up with a broken nose and another with a broken arm, but they had won.

With efficient and unhurried movements, he assembled the MK 15. Just as he put the final piece in place and snapped in a magazine, movement on the edge of his vision made him look up at the ridgetop.

His pursuer had made it. Damn, that man was fast. Not only that, but he was also smart. He hadn't followed Operative 313 through the crevasse he had gone through, or the one next to it. He had angled to the north with the speed of a mountain goat and come through a third, narrower crevasse.

Operative 313 only saw him for a second, but that was enough to sign the stranger's death warrant.

The guy was definitely following him, not as a spy but as a hunter. No one takes that much care on a recon.

Operative 313 went prone, squirming into a tight spot between a boulder and a thorn bush that jabbed at his shoulder and cheek but provided the cover he needed. Resting the rifle on its bipod, he looked through the scope and adjusted the range to 1,400 meters.

Once that was set, he scanned back and forth across the ridgeline. He did not expect to see his pursuer, not yet. Instead, he searched for places where he could.

There, about a third of the way between where the pursuer had jumped across the ridge and the crevasse that he himself had taken. There was a clear patch where no boulders stood, and no bushes clung to the rock. It had obviously been made by that slab of stone lying fifty meters below, which weathering had finally pried from its perch to send tumbling down until it got caught on a ledge. It had taken all cover with it for a width of two meters.

If the guy correctly assumed Operative 313's original intention of staying in the crevasse until the sun rose higher, he'd cross along the ridge, dart across that narrow space, and sneak up on the crevasse to give his quarry a nasty surprise.

Two meters, at a range of 1,400 meters, against a man who would almost certainly be sprinting. He'd have to fire the instant he became visible, or the bullet wouldn't reach him in time.

Operative 313 did the math. The bullet from his rifle had a muzzle velocity of 823 meters per second, meaning at this range the bullet would take almost two seconds to reach the target.

Too long. The guy would have passed by the open space by then.

He continued to search with his scope, powerful optics bringing every detail of the distant ridge close and clear.

There, just before the open space on the most obvious route across the ridge, was a fissure in a rock behind which the stranger would have to pass. The sun shone right through it. He'd make a brief shadow as he passed.

The guy would remain visible for far too brief a time to make a shot, but if Operative 313 timed it right, and aimed for the far side of the eroded area, he might just tag the guy.

Assuming he took that route. Assuming he didn't pause before he bolted across the open space. Assuming he ran as fast as Operative 313 thought he would. Assuming Operative 313 could hit him even if all those other factors fell into place.

That last assumption was the only one Operative 313 had confidence in.

This had better work. Only one shot would make it hard for anyone in the valley to pinpoint. He didn't dare take a second one, and the guy was too good to give him that chance. It would be better not to take the shot at all and bushwhack his pursuer in a quieter fight with his Bowie knife, but he didn't have the time. He had a rendezvous with some friendlies that he couldn't be late for.

He took the time to make a couple of practice sweeps from the cleft in the rock where he would spot the guy to the point on the far end of the eroded space where he would fire. Back and forth, back and forth until he had the movement down. Then he focused on the cleft, let out a long, slow breath, and waited.

Operative 313 only had to wait for a few more seconds.

A dark flash in the cleft. Made it there already? This guy was mountain born and bred, that was for sure. Operative 313 moved his sights to the far end of the eroded area and pulled the trigger. A loud crack sounded through the valley, the sound waves moving toward the target as the target moved toward the bullet racing to intercept him. The bullet would make it before the sound, silent death followed too late by the warning.

And there he was, right on cue, a man in a gray shalwar kameez and pakoi hat of brown wool, an AK and leather satchel slung over his shoulder.

Just before he disappeared behind the boulder at the far side of the eroded strip, he spun like a top, blood spurting from a wound to the side. The man tumbled, head over heels, down the eroded area for several meters before coming to a sprawling stop, head facing down the slope, legs splayed.

Operative 313 waited. The gritty soil around the target blackened, the stain spreading downslope. The man did not move. He lay at an angle where his wounds were not visible, but judging by the movement of the stain, the heavy round had pierced his side and gone right through, smashing both sides of the rib cage and probably taking out a couple of internal organs on its way.

No way the guy was shamming death. Operative 313 scanned the ridge for signs of a second man he might have missed but saw none. His pursuer had been an assassin, working alone.

He took a good look around the valley and saw no movement. Someone was bound to have heard that shot. The clear mountain air would have carried the sound for miles. But no one seemed eager to investigate.

Better hurry anyway. Operative 313 stripped and stowed his rifle in record time, packed up, and raced up to check on the man he had killed.

He stopped several times on the way to check the valley. It remained as still as a grave.

When he made it to the body, he got a surprise. This man wasn't Afghani or Pakistani as his clothes would suggest. He was Kashmiri.

Kashmir was a mostly Muslim region in northwestern India that had a large popular movement to leave the majority Hindu nation and join with Muslim Pakistan. Pakistan funded insurgents there in a nasty proxy war that had been going on for a couple of generations.

What was a Kashmiri doing here? And why was he hunting him? A few had joined the jihad against the Soviet invaders in the 1980s, and against the American invaders in the early 2000s, but nowadays, they all set their sights on the Indian army.

He rummaged through the man's pockets, coming up with a wad of Pakistani rupees worth at least $1,000 and a Pakistani national ID that looked real but was almost certainly fake. In the satchel, he found a load of plastic explosives and detonators. He took that, dragged the body behind a rock, and got out of sight himself.

Hunkered down in the shade between two stones, he considered his situation. That the man had been hunting him personally he had no doubt. So, who had sent him, and why did he have plastic explosives? Had the Kashmiri planned to make a trap and blow him up? Possibly.

But who sent him? Al-Qaeda, the Taliban, or the local branch of ISIS would have sent a group after him, not a single assassin, and almost certainly not a Kashmiri. Plus, they had shown no sign of being able to track his movements. He'd been eluding them all for months now.

That left only one other option, the worst option of all.

The Order. Somehow the Order, with its vast tentacles in all theaters of operations, had located him.

And if the Order was on his ass, he'd have to be very, very careful.

Because as good as he was, this Kashmiri lying at his feet wasn't nearly the worst thing they could throw at him.

CHAPTER SIX

Madrid, Spain
The next day

Jacob looked around at the crowd of Madrid's busy Rastro antique market. Held every Sunday for more than two centuries, it was a vast collection of temporary stalls and regular shops selling everything from eighteenth century furniture to movie magazines from the 1950s. Every week when the stalls were set up for a day, the Rastro attracted vast throngs of tourists and locals.

Big crowds always put Jacob on high alert. They made prime targets for terrorist attacks and excellent venues for spies to tail them.

He knew he was being paranoid. No one knew he and Jana were here or why they had come. He had told his boss Tyler Wallace he was taking some time off to enjoy some Spanish cooking, something he loved, and Wallace had believed him. Probably. It was hard to slip something by that guy.

But if they were being watched, it was by a friendly, so Jacob had no reason to be nervous as he scanned the crowd of passive faces smiling in the sun, or the rows of stalls selling colorful bullfighting posters, vintage postcards, and stacks of old leather-bound volumes.

And yet he watched. He had seen too much, survived too much, not to.

"The shop is down the next street on the left, I think," Jana said.

Efficient and resourceful as usual, Jacob thought.

Being with Jana again felt good, although at the same time, it also made him feel even more guilty about what happened to Gabriella. He didn't understand that, and he wasn't about to delve into it. He had a mission to accomplish. If Wallace wouldn't let him hunt for the people responsible for the bomb, at least he could take out some different bad guys.

The place was a maze of streets flanked by old, brick buildings with ironwork balconies or more elaborate façades with plaster ornamentation painted white or canary yellow, brilliant in the Spanish sun.

The goal in this maze was the antiquarian bookshop of Inez Domingo, a colleague of the murdered Antonio Vasquez. Jana had tracked down several articles they had written together on old maps for specialty magazines. Most recently, Señora Domingo had written a eulogy on a collectors' website about Vasquez, recalling a long friendship and collaboration.

She sounded like a potentially cooperative and helpful informant. They hoped she could provide some leads.

But they had to proceed carefully. She could have been in on the murder, or she could be another target. Jacob and Jana still knew far too little to make any assumptions in relation to this case.

They continued down one of the narrower streets. The stalls hemmed them in to either side, the crowd growing thicker. Jacob kept scanning.

Then he saw a well-dressed, older gentleman with a white goatee in front of him and a little to the right. His movements looked suspicious. He was tailing a wealthy-looking woman carrying a big purse, coming up close behind her. With a deft movement, he unclasped it and put his hand inside.

Jacob took two quick steps through the press of people, grabbed the man's fingers, twisted, and dislocated one. The man cried out, but Jacob was already gone, back beside Jana.

"What happened?" she asked as the pickpocket let out a wail of anguish and people gathered around to stare.

"Performing a bit of civic duty," Jacob said. "Keep walking."

He had no fear the pickpocket would narc on him. What would he say? "This guy attacked me while I was trying to steal that woman's money?" Not likely.

"There it is," Jana said, pointing to a narrow shopfront whose windows were adorned with old books and maps. "Try not to get us into any more trouble, all right?"

"I stop trouble, not cause it."

Jana snorted. "Tell me another one."

"Whatever. You remember how we're going to play this?"

"Yes."

"Let's do it."

Jacob took a final look at the crowd, didn't see any obvious tails, and entered the shop. A little bell above the door tinkled.

They came into a small room of two aisles filled with books. All of them looked old, some centuries so. The walls were adorned with antique engravings and maps, and at the far end stood a row of drawers labeled with various geographical locations. Probably more of the map collection.

An elderly gentleman stood in one of the aisles flipping through a hundred-year-old medical encyclopedia. At a desk near the map case sat a middle-aged woman with wavy, black hair and a brilliant, amber necklace that looked real. A heavy, gold ring with a sparkling emerald adorned one of her fingers. Apparently, the book and map business were profitable ones.

"Señora Domingo?" he asked as he came up to the desk.

"Yes. How may I help you?"

Jacob pulled out his Interpol ID. He wasn't actually in Interpol, but it was a good fake, and it wasn't like this bookseller was going to check.

"Jacob Snow. Interpol. We need to ask you a few questions about Antonio Vasquez."

Her face fell. "What a tragedy. Of course, I'll help, but I've already told the municipal police everything I know."

"We have a few different questions, madam."

All this was said in Spanish, hers in high-class Castilian, his with the rougher tones of the dockside Mediterranean bars where he had learned the language, and a few tricks in knife fighting as an educational bonus.

Inez Domingo stood, apologized to the elderly customer, and got him out of the store. She locked the door, flipped the sign from open to closed, and turned to them.

"So, what do two Interpol agents want to know about my poor friend's murder?"

Jacob suppressed a smile at her assumption that Jana was his partner. He knew that Jana wouldn't have to produce an ID. Civilians were always a bit overwhelmed when faced with the law and never asked awkward questions.

"We were wondering if Señor Vasquez had anything in his collection that would attract organized crime," Jana probed.

"Organized crime? What would … oh, I see. You mean forgeries. No, he was always honest in his dealings."

Jacob wasn't a hundred percent sure of that, although he had no evidence to the contrary.

"Anything of special note that got stolen? We have an itemized list, but we were curious to hear your insights."

43

"Many of the prints and maps were quite valuable. Señor Vasquez kept detailed records, so we know exactly what's missing, and the total retail value is worth more than 30,000 euros." Her gaze fell. Tears welled in her eye. "Killing such a kind and brilliant man for 30,000 euros. I don't know what this world is coming to."

"We're sorry for your loss," Jana said. "We were interested in one particular item, a map of the coast of Venezuela from the late eighteenth century signed by a mapmaker named Joaquino."

The antiquarian bookseller looked up in surprise. "That thing? That's the least valuable item that was stolen."

"Why's that?" Jacob asked.

"Because it's a fake."

That's what the pirate said.

Jacob feigned surprise. "Really? How do you know?"

"It's a copy of an earlier map purportedly showing a shipwreck full of treasure. There is no such shipwreck according to the records. And it's not even an original. It's a copy of the fake. I suppose you're investigating Señor Barrado's murder down in Malaga, yes?"

"We are."

"The police asked me about that since men both collected old maps and had some stolen. He had a copy of the same map. It was a fake too."

That really did catch Jacob by surprise. "Really? How can you know?"

"For a long time, it was purported to be the real copy and many sources name it as such, but recent research has shown that not to be the case."

Jacob smiled. So, the pirates didn't have the real one? God, he hoped not. Good news was rare on a mission.

"Has this recent research been published anywhere?"

"No, but it was the subject of a speech at the Royal Spanish Cartography Association a few months ago."

"Who gave this speech?"

Señora Domingo got a look like she had just sucked on a lemon. "David Pérez. He's a wealthy collector living in Brunete. He, too, has a copy of the treasure map, and he proved convincingly that his was the real copy. Vasquez and I both attended the meeting, and we were both swayed by his arguments."

"Is Señor Pérez reputable?" Jana asked, picking up on the bookseller's negative body language.

"Well, he's a good scholar, I'll give him that," Domingo grumbled. "But he's a snake. He earned his fortune developing real estate. There was a huge real estate bubble here in Spain a few years ago. He was responsible for a lot of it. Bribing corrupt mayors of small towns for rezoning, ignoring environmental laws, duping speculators into investing in housing estates that would never be profitable, tricking regular people with promises of luxurious housing developments that would never be finished. He wasn't the only one doing this, but he was the worst. The country was left with vast unfinished estates that ended up as ghost towns. Those foolish enough to invest lost everything. The newspapers say it led to tens of thousands of bankruptcies."

"Did he ever stand trial?" Jacob asked.

"Ha! People like that never stand trial. It was all buried behind shell corporations and legalese. He and his cronies crippled this country's economy for years." She looked at him, a sudden worry crossing her face. "But I don't think he murdered my two colleagues. Please don't think that. Pérez is a corrupt, greedy bastard, but he is no murderer. Besides, he has the real map. Why would he steal the fake ones?"

"Good point," Jacob said. *Unless Pérez is running some sort of scam with that talk of his to deflect suspicion. He sounds capable of it.*

"I think we should talk to him in any case," Jana said. "Do you have his contact information?"

"Certainly. I've done some business with him, although I prefer not to. I'll give you his number and email."

"His address, too, please," Jacob said.

As she fetched the information, Jacob checked his phone to find Brunete. It turned out to be a small town thirty kilometers east of Madrid. Good. Maybe they could get this done quickly.

When the bookseller returned with a piece of paper with Pérez's contact information and address, Jacob and Jana thanked her and left.

"This man sounds like he's going to be uncooperative," Jana said as they headed down the busy street. "How are we going to convince him to part with his map?"

"We're not," Jacob said. "We're going to steal it."

CHAPTER SEVEN

Jana didn't like the idea of stealing a map, not even from a scummy businessman like David Pérez. Lives could be on the line, though, and that was the only consideration Jacob thought of.

They had argued, and he had won. With relentless logic, he had explained that taking a photo of the map—assuming the real estate developer would let them—wouldn't be enough. What if there was some detail they couldn't see except under ideal light? What if there was something on the back or covered by the frame? What if they needed to accurately measure portions of the map and compare it to a modern chart?

And they couldn't ask to borrow it, not with someone like that. He'd only think it was more valuable and demand a price they couldn't afford.

Jacob was right. Damn that man.

Jacob Snow was like a robot, his mind working on only one task— to finish the mission. Nothing else mattered. No one else mattered.

God, how she hated that attitude. She had gotten her fill of it from her father.

They drove a rental car along a country road near the town of Brunete, the last golden glimmerings of the setting sun playing off a castle sitting atop a rocky eminence. A few farms and holiday homes stood scattered across a landscape of gentle hills. Pérez's mansion stood a couple of kilometers ahead.

She had called the businessman saying she was a collector from the United States passing through Madrid and was interested in seeing what items he had for sale. A secretary had answered the phone and at first tried to get rid of her.

"Señor Pérez doesn't like doing business on a Sunday."

Yeah, a real religious guy. Jana wasn't dissuaded. She had persisted, saying she was flying back to New York the following day, and at last, after a long time waiting on hold, the secretary had relented.

She noticed Jacob kept glancing in the direction of the distant castle.

"What is it?" she said, searching the open fields and a nearby olive orchard for movement.

"That castle. The walls look like they've been hit by artillery rounds."

Jana shook her head. "My God, do you ever switch off?"

"No. That's why I'm still alive."

Just like Dad. On his rare visits home when he'd take her to the beach or a fun fair, those eyes were always roving, searching, checking. Looking at everything else but her. She wasn't a threat, so she didn't get Dad's attention.

No, this irritating man sitting next to her got all of that.

"That really looks like small-bore artillery damage," Jacob insisted.

"I suppose it is. This was a battlefield during the Spanish Civil War when Franco's fascists advanced on Madrid."

"Oh," Jacob said, losing interest and looking back at the road. "I wonder if our collector friend is a fascist."

"We'll soon find out. It's just another kilometer. Time for you to get out."

The plan was for Jana to go in posing as a buyer and string Pérez along while Jacob broke in, found the map, and took it. Inez Domingo had given them a clear enough description that they could spot it. The problem was, if it was kept with all the other maps, Pérez and Jana might be sitting in that same room.

If that was the case, they'd have to figure out a workaround.

Jacob parked the car on the gravel shoulder of the narrow country lane and got out. By the time Jana had eased over to the driver's seat, he had already disappeared into the bushes.

"Good luck to you, too," she grumbled and got the car into gear.

Her anger at him was tinged with concern. He still moved stiffly from his injuries and was obviously in discomfort. Would he be able to manage the physical demands his half of this job required of him?

He needed to angle through the field and find a way inside the mansion, which from Google Earth looked like an old-style, stone hacienda with extensive grounds surrounded by a wall. Street View didn't cover a place this rural, so they had no other intel.

Jana drove the final kilometer to where the road dead-ended at an iron gate flanked by a smooth, stone wall ten feet tall. A security camera pointed down at her. She couldn't see more cameras around the perimeter, but she bet they were there. A metal stand with a buzzer and intercom stood in front of the gate. She opened the car window and pressed it.

A male voice came over the intercom. "Ms. Anderson?"

"Yes."

Jill Anderson. That was the alias she had picked for herself. She wished she was better dressed for the part. She hadn't brought any fine clothes or jewelry on this trip and had only managed to buy a reasonably suitable outfit in Madrid at the last minute.

The gate clicked, then swung open automatically.

"Come through the main drive and park next to the fountain."

She drove slowly through the gate and found herself on a broad front lawn. The grass was a bit brown, and the bushes needed tending. Spain had suffered a drought in recent months, and Pérez hadn't been watering his massive yard. She doubted it was due to any concerns for the environment. He probably just didn't care.

The hacienda appearing before her was a different story. A massive, two-story stone structure with columns in front of the main door and two large wings, it looked to date to the nineteenth century and was well maintained. A circular drive ran around it, with a splashing fountain of white marble showing Poseidon riding a dolphin flanked by Nereids.

As she parked beside it, Jana did a double take. The fountain was Roman. Here and there it had been restored where pieces had been lost in the past two thousand years, but the bulk of it was original. Jana couldn't even begin to calculate how much Pérez must have spent to buy it.

Jana got out, the front door of the hacienda opened, and a pair of immense Dobermans shot out, snarling and coming straight for her.

She shrieked and grabbed the door handle, ready to jump back inside the car. A sharp whistle from the doorway brought the Dobermans up short, barely ten feet from her. Another sharp whistle, and they paced back to the front door.

A man stood there, who Jana recognized from an Internet search as David Pérez.

He had the refined features of old money, with swept-back salt and pepper hair, an erect bearing, and powerful hands. Jana guessed his age at about fifty, but his body was that of a younger man. He obviously took care of himself. She wouldn't be surprised if he had a personal trainer and a full gym somewhere on the grounds. Google Earth showed an Olympic-sized swimming pool in the backyard.

"Ms. Anderson, how good of you to come," Pérez said in a cultured English that spoke of a British public-school education. "I am always eager to meet another aficionado of early cartography."

Now came the tricky part. Jana actually knew relatively little about early maps. She decided to stick to her specialty and hope she could carry the conversation that way.

"I was just admiring your fountain. Second century, I believe?"

Pérez raised a heavy eyebrow. "Ah, you have a love of the Classical civilizations as well. Yes, second century. It came from a villa in southeast France."

"Most impressive," she said, taking a few steps toward the front door and then hesitating. The Dobermans stood flanking their master, gazing at her with a hungry look.

"Oh, I do apologize." He snapped his fingers, and they disappeared into the house. "Don't worry about them. They only attack on command, or if they discover an intruder."

"Not a problem. Oh, pardon me, my phone is buzzing."

She pulled out her phone and sent a text to Jacob, saying only: "Dogs."

Then she put her phone away, her hands shaking a little, hoping he checked his phone before making the final approach.

When she turned back to Pérez, she caught him looking her over, and not in a way that a man usually looks over a woman. He was taking in the details of her modest dress, mid-priced shoes, and lack of jewelry. "Jill Anderson" did not look like a rich collector.

Then again, Americans had a reputation in Europe for being underdressed. Jana hoped her knowledge would carry her through.

"Was it one of the villas outside Lugdunum?" Jana asked, coming up the steps and shaking his hand. He had a firm grip and, surprisingly, his palm was calloused.

"A little more to the south, but on the main road from Lugdunum to the coast. Come. May I offer you tea or coffee?"

"Thank you, no. I'm afraid I haven't much time."

They entered a spacious front hall, the walls adorned with old portraits, a traditional Virgin and Child that looked seventeenth century, and a floor of Italian marble.

"Yes, you mentioned that. Then let's get straight down to business. This way."

He led her through an open doorway to the left, through a sumptuous but soulless living room of antique gilded furniture, and into a spacious study. The walls were covered with maps of all descriptions and periods, and a long row of map drawers took up one side. A large worktable, fitted with more map drawers, stood at the center of the room.

"So, what is of interest to you? My personal assistant didn't give me many details. Most of my collection is negotiable, except for a few items."

"I'm very interested in early maps on archaeological subjects, and I'm also looking for a gift for my brother. He's fascinated with maritime history, especially of the Caribbean."

David Pérez's face lit up. "Ah! That is a special interest of mine. As you can see from the walls, I have quite the collection of maritime maps."

Jana studied them, making impressed noises she did not have to feign. She noticed that most of the nautical maps were of the Caribbean Sea and Barbary Coast from the seventeenth to early nineteenth centuries, a high time for piracy.

"You seem to have an interest in pirates, Señor Pérez."

The millionaire real estate developer laughed. "In every man, a little boy still lives inside, and as a man of my means, I am able to indulge myself."

Jana smiled. "I think you and my brother would get along."

Pérez inclined his head. "Come this way. I'd like to show you something that your brother would appreciate. It isn't for sale, but you can tell him about it."

Jana knew she had hit the jackpot. She had met many collectors in her life, and they could never resist showing off the best of their collection. Pérez led her back through the main hall, through a large dining room featuring a huge, oak table, and into a more modern living room in the east wing, with comfortable furnishings and a pricey home entertainment system.

And there, above the sofa, hung the map that everyone was making such a fuss over.

Jana recognized it instantly thanks to the bookseller's description. She studied it for a moment as Pérez proudly told her about it.

"This map was drawn in 1768 and purports to show the wreck of the *Santo Santiago*, an infamous pirate ship of the time. They had attacked a colony ship called the *Nueva Esperanza* and plundered it. They didn't kill the people on board, but reports say they took absolutely everything that could have been of even the smallest value, even their food. The colony ship was lucky to make it back to port before everyone starved. Shortly thereafter, the *Santo Santiago* sank as well. As you can see, the coordinates are quite precise."

"*Santo Santiago*. Saint James. An odd name for a pirate ship."

"The crew hailed from northern Spain, through which the famous pilgrimage route of the Camino Santiago runs. Sailors are a superstitious lot, and they often call on Divine intervention. Even pirates."

"Are you going to look for it?"

"I'm researching the possibility right now. It's a major undertaking and requires a great deal of groundwork. Still, it is a dream of mine."

"How did the *Santo Santiago* sink?" Jana asked.

"It's unclear. Not by a naval ship, otherwise there would be an official record. The cartographer who made this map, Teo Joaquino, had an accompanying text to go with it, but sadly that has been lost to time. I've searched every archive and private collection I could access. There is simply no record of how the *Santo Santiago* went down."

"A storm?"

"Perhaps. Or perhaps by a rival. It happened sometimes. We know that another pirate ship, the *Vengeance*, was in the area."

Jana's skin prickled. Jacob had shown her the transcript of the intercepted conversation, and it appeared the modern pirate ship was also named the *Vengeance*. That couldn't be a coincidence.

"My brother would love this. A pity it isn't for sale."

"Sorry. Let's go back to the map room, and I'll show you some things that you and your brother would be interested in."

"May I take a photo of this?"

He raised a broad hand. "Sorry but no. I'm sure you understand."

They turned to head back. A butler passed by them in the hall, his muscular body bulging in his uniform.

"May I use the restroom?" Jana asked. "It was a long drive."

"Of course. Francisco, show Ms. Anderson the restroom and then bring her to the map room. In the meantime, I will lay out a few things that might be of interest."

The butler, who looked more like a bodyguard, led her a short way down the hall to a restroom. Jana entered and pulled out her phone. Her initial message hadn't been received. Jana bit her lip. She sent a second one.

"Map is in the modern living room just off main hall in east wing."

She hoped he'd read both before he got into trouble.

Jana waited for another minute, flushed the toilet, ran the sink, and then came out of the restroom. Francisco was still waiting outside.

Big surprise. Señor Pérez was not about to allow her the freedom to wander through his mansion.

Francisco escorted her back to the map room and withdrew. Pérez stood by the worktable, several maritime maps laid out before him. He was just opening a folder full of maps from early nineteenth-century archaeological reports.

"Here we have a fine selection of—"

His voice got cut off by furious barking somewhere inside the house.

CHAPTER EIGHT

Jana's heart leapt to her throat. David Pérez cast her a suspicious look and called out in Spanish.

"Francisco! Luis! Go find out what's going on."

Oh great, there's a second bodyguard.

Jana stood there for a moment, unsure what to do. The barking continued, and she heard the sound of thundering footsteps. The collector turned to her.

"Don't be afraid of the dogs. They sense someone on the grounds. We've had prowlers before. Usually leftist protestors from Madrid. We'll soon scare them off."

While his words sounded reassuring, his eyes continued to carry the glint of suspicion. After all, she had shown up with no references and here was an intruder arriving right at the same time.

There was a loud crash of breaking wood. Pérez cursed and moved to a desk on the far side of the room. From the top drawer, he pulled out an old revolver.

"What are you doing?" Jana cried.

Her words were nearly drowned out by the sound of a loud thud, as of a body hitting a solid surface.

"Protecting my property. What do you think?"

"I thought handguns were illegal in Spain."

"A common misperception. It is merely difficult due to paperwork and permissions. Stay here and lock the door. I'll call out when all is safe."

He hurried out of the room, closing the door behind him.

Jana had no intention of staying where she was. She moved over to the door. She listened for a moment and, hearing nothing but the continued barking, opened the door a crack and peeked out.

A large man thundered past, heading down the hallway. Jana closed the door. That must have been the second bodyguard.

She needed to get that map, but first she needed to figure out where the action was.

She checked her phone. Jacob hadn't read her messages. The idiot was probably in the wrong part of the house.

Bad for him, good for her. If she was careful, she might just be able to sneak in and grab the map.

What she'd do then was still a matter for conjecture.

She peeked out again. The coast was clear. She darted across the main hall, through the dining room, and into the living room.

Just as she did, she heard someone cry out. It sounded like Jacob, but it was too distant for her to be sure.

More sounds of fighting. She didn't worry too much. Jacob had taken on unfair odds plenty of times. She just hoped Pérez didn't get trigger happy. She didn't know if Jacob was carrying or not, but she sure didn't want this to devolve into a gunfight.

She moved up to the map and lifted it off the wall.

The instant she did so, an alarm started screeching.

Whoops.

She ran out of the living room and into the dining room, gripping the map and heading for the front door. Halfway across the dining room, she came to an abrupt halt as the two Dobermans rounded the corner and, teeth bared, came straight for her.

She turned with a yelp and sprinted back into the living room, slamming the door behind her.

A moment later, two huge, canine bodies crashed into the door with a bang. The wood around the lock splintered, and Jana only just managed to push the door shut again before the dogs swarmed inside.

She leaned her back against it, clutching the framed map to her chest, the siren still wailing. The dogs slammed into it a second time. She braced her legs and kept them back. Then she heard their claws clacking on the tile floor as they ran off.

For a moment, she was confused. She hadn't heard anyone call them off.

Then she saw the two open doors on the other walls of the room.

Those dogs know the house better than I do.

Jana glanced at the window. Locked. No time to open it.

She raced for the first door and saw it opened into a hallway. She slammed it shut. That would buy her all of about half a second. Then she ran for the far door and saw it opened into a restroom. She closed and locked the door behind her and got to work opening the narrow window.

Just as she got it open and swung her leg over the sash, the door crashed open.

The bodyguard named Francisco stood there, glowering. He reached for her …

Jana tipped herself over the sash to land in a flowerbed. She rolled away, thorns clawing at her. Rose bushes. But of course, they'd be.

She sprang to her feet, covered in a dozen cuts, leaving large patches of her dress behind. Francisco got to the window and shouted something at her she didn't catch, his muscular body too big to make it through the window.

Then he disappeared back inside.

Not much time. She ran for the car, coming around the corner of the house and angling across the front lawn to head for where it was parked next to the Roman fountain.

She almost made it when the front door opened. Francisco stood there. The two Dobermans leapt past him and charged at her.

Jana picked up speed, trying to estimate if she or those loping masses of muscles and teeth would make it to the car first. She wasn't sure. A quick glance showed them bearing down on her, Francisco coming up behind, then she focused on running.

If you're trying to run away from someone, her father always said, *keep your eyes on where you're going. Don't keep looking at them to see if they're catching up. It breaks your stride and slows you down.*

Don't keep looking at them? Easier said than done. She saw the sense in it, though. No point looking. They would either catch up, or they wouldn't.

They didn't. She got to the car, tore open the door, hopped in so quickly she knocked her head, tossed the map into the back seat, and slammed the door behind her.

A moment later, one of the Dobermans banged into the window, cracking it. Jana fumbled for her keys as the two dogs jumped around the car, barking their heads off.

Just as she got her key into the ignition, the car door opened.

Francisco. In her haste, she had forgotten to lock the door. He grabbed her arm and started to haul her out.

With her free hand, she turned on the ignition, put the car into gear, and stepped on the gas.

This had two opposite effects. It sent the car forward and sent her back as Francisco held on with an iron grip.

He got her out enough that her foot came off the gas. The car slowed.

The eyes, Dad always said. *The eyes are weak. It doesn't matter how big the guy is.*

She took her free hand off the wheel, forked her fingers, and jabbed them into Francisco's eyes. Her own violence made her cringe in disgust.

The bodyguard cried out, clutching his eyes with both hands.

That gave her all the chance she needed. She hit the gas, ducked to the side as one of the Dobermans put its head inside the car and snapped at her, and tore down the driveway.

She closed the door and picked up speed, the dogs loping behind her. Francisco recovered after a moment and ran after the car, too, murder in his red, tearing eyes.

If they can lock the gate remotely, I'm not sure what I'm going to do.

She screeched to a halt in front of the iron gate. A pillar with a button stood next to the road. She opened her window and hit the button.

A moment later, she had to pull back as one of the Dobermans leapt at her hand, coming an inch from tearing it off.

She hit the button to close the window. The other Doberman stuck its head in and snapped at her hand. Again, she had to pull away. The Doberman got its front legs into the car, its hot breath wafting in her face. Lying almost prone, Jana hit reverse. The dog snarled and barked, but the motion of the car made him jump back out.

Jana kept reversing, closing the window as she did so. The dogs pursued her back the way she came.

In the rearview mirror, she saw Francisco looming up behind.

The gate was opening. She stopped, switched into drive, and hit the gas. Francisco grabbed onto the rear of the car, stumbled, and let go.

Jana sped toward the gate, which was opening with agonizing slowness. She gritted her teeth and kept going, aiming right for the center of the widening aperture.

There was a bang as she passed through. Both sideview mirrors had vanished. Jana tried to remember if Jacob had bought insurance. Probably not, knowing him.

She picked up more speed as she drove down the rural lane. The dogs ran after her until they dwindled out of sight in the rearview mirror.

Now what? Francisco and the others would pursue. They might have captured Jacob, but even if they hadn't, with the map gone their number one target would be her now.

And the road to and from the hacienda was long and straight with no side roads for at least a couple of miles. They might catch up to her before she had a chance to take a side road and try to shake them.

And what about Jacob? She couldn't leave him back there.

Her phone rang. She grabbed it. Jacob!

She answered. Before she could say anything, Jacob cut her off.

"Did you get it?" he was whispering.

"Yeah. That's what set off the alarm. Where are you?"

"Managed to get out of the house. Had a hell of a fight with some guy named Luis. I'm sneaking through an olive grove right now. I think they're still after me."

"Watch out for the dogs. They chased me out the gate, but they're probably heading home now."

"All right. I'm angling toward the road. Try to meet me at—"

His voice got cut off by the sound of gunfire.

"Jacob! Are you all right?"

The phone cut off.

CHAPTER NINE

Jacob ducked behind an olive tree as the bullets from Pérez's revolver splintered the wood. His pursuer was still a good thirty yards back, a tough range for a revolver through partial cover, but Pérez didn't show any signs of giving up, and Luis, one of the bodyguards, was out here somewhere too.

Jacob bolted from the dubious cover of one olive tree to another. Pérez didn't fire, running forward to reduce the range between them instead.

At least Jana was safe. Hopefully, she could meet him at the road somewhere.

A movement to his right caught his eye. Luis. He hoped that hunk of muscle and aggressiveness didn't have a gun. After knocking one of Luis's teeth out, that Spanish thug wasn't going to be in a charitable mood.

A shot from that direction told him that Spain's strict gun laws didn't apply to people like Luis.

Jacob ducked low and zigzagged between the olive trees, wishing they were oaks instead. Olive trees were too thin and small to make adequate cover.

Another shot ploughed up the soil inches in front of his feet. Whether it was from Luis or Pérez, he didn't know. He kept his head down and focused on running.

The ridiculous thing about this whole affair was that he was packing. He had a slim model 9mm automatic in a shoulder holster hidden under his vest. While Pérez showed some skill with a gun, and Luis looked ex-military, he could take out these two guys no problem.

But he couldn't. While these guys weren't what you'd call squeaky clean, he couldn't link them to any crime. In fact, they were the victims here. That bullet whizzing overhead close enough to part his hair counted as self-defense.

Not that Jacob felt guilty about robbing them. If those pirates really were trying to find a deadly virus culture, then a little breaking and entering didn't count for much. He'd done a lot worse in the cause of world peace and democracy. He promised to give Pérez back his precious map once all this was said and done.

If he could get off the property first. If they could stop the pirates. If he and Jana got back from the mission alive.

Those ifs sure were mounting up. He saw the boundary wall ahead, and it was way too smooth and high for him to scale.

Another bullet cracking off an olive tree made him duck to the left, and there he saw something that might just save him.

A long pole with a pruning hook on the end, leaning against one of the trees, obviously forgotten by some careless groundskeeper.

He grabbed it, knowing his next move was a stupid idea. But hey, "stupid idea" was practically his middle name.

Jacob "Stupid Idea" Snow raced toward the wall, clutching the end of the pole, keeping the sharp edge of the pruning hook facing away from him.

He judged the distance, ignoring the bullet that sang past him to chip the stone wall.

Just before he hit the wall himself, he jabbed the blunt end of the pole into the soil and jumped. The pole swung up, and he pole vaulted right over the wall.

In his dreams. Instead, his sprained wrist yelped with pain, and he almost lost his grip. He certainly lost some momentum, and that made his knees hit the top of the wall, and he toppled over the other side, landing hard on his wrist.

His bad wrist. Because of course it would be his bad wrist.

He took a moment to lie there swearing and moaning. Pérez and Luis were stuck on the other side. He could spare a few moments to cry like a baby.

Clutching his throbbing wrist, still swearing, and allowing himself the occasional moan, he got up and staggered for the road he could just see through the sparse vegetation.

As he got to the roadside, Jana pulled up and screeched to a halt.

"Fancy meeting you here," he said with a grin.

"Get in. They'll be after us in a second."

Jacob landed in the passenger's seat with a relieved sigh. "Did you get it? Please say you got it."

"I got it. Now we have to get away."

She swung the car around and peeled out.

"What happened to the side view mirrors?"

"Don't ask."

"And why is the window cracked?"

"Don't ask. Did you buy insurance?"

"Don't ask."

They sped down the country road.

"I remember an intersection a couple of miles up. Take a turn," Jacob said.

"Which way?"

"Who cares? We just got to get off this road. Straight ahead leads to the highway back to Madrid, and they know that's the way we came."

Jana tried to speed up, but the underpowered rental didn't go nearly as fast as Jacob would like.

Jana glanced at him. "You all right?"

"Sure. Why wouldn't I be?"

"You're holding your wrist and gritting your teeth in pain."

"Oh, that. Yeah, I pole vaulted over the wall and landed on my injured wrist."

"I didn't know they taught pole vaulting in the CIA."

"They don't. I just sort of imitated what I've seen on TV. Did pretty good. Didn't stick the landing though."

Jana looked in the rearview mirror and went pale. Jacob looked over his shoulder and saw a Mercedes roaring up behind them. The sound of its souped-up engine grew louder.

"Crap," Jacob said.

"What do we do? We'll never outrace them."

The passenger window lowered, and Luis leaned out of the window, a gun in his hand.

"Double crap," Jacob said, rolling down his own window.

Jana swerved just as Luis fired, then swerved back again as he took a second shot.

"Who taught you evasive driving?" Jacob asked.

"Who do you think?"

"OK. Don't get too crazy."

Jacob leaned out the window, holding his 9mm with his left hand, his off hand. He couldn't hold anything with his right, not even the windowsill, so he braced his elbow against the windowsill and hoped Jana wouldn't zigzag so much that he'd topple out.

Luis got off another round that shattered the back window. Jana let out a cry.

Jacob didn't have time to see if she was hurt. He aimed and fired at the pursuing car's engine block.

A miss.

The Mercedes drew closer. Luis looked right at him and aimed.

Jacob fired first, again aiming for the engine block.

A direct hit. Sparks flew from the grill, and the driver swerved, making Luis's shot go wide. Steam began to billow out from around the hood.

Jacob didn't dare risk another shot at the engine. He didn't want to hit the gas line and set the whole thing up in a fireball. Instead, he fired at the front tire, missed, fired a second time, and missed again.

By then it didn't matter. The Mercedes was lurching to a halt, its engine letting out all sorts of nasty grinding sounds.

Jacob slipped back into his seat, and right on top of a mass of broken glass.

"Ouch!" Jacob said, pulling up his butt and wiping the glass onto the floor.

"Ouch yourself," Jana said. "Pick this glass out of my hair."

Jacob holstered his pistol, took a final look in the rearview mirror to make sure no one else was following them, and did as he was asked.

"You're cut a bit," Jacob said, finding little drops of blood on the back of her neck.

"You think I don't know that?" Jana snapped.

"What are you angry at me for?"

"What do you think?"

Jacob stared at her. Jana glanced at him, did a double take, and her frown deepened.

"You really don't know, do you?"

"Um, no. We got the map. You're not badly hurt. Hell, I'm way more hurt than you are and I'm not complaining."

"Jesus! We committed breaking and entering, stole private property, destroyed someone's car, and wrecked a rental car."

"Oh, we don't have to pay for that. I used fake ID. We'll ditch it in Madrid and take a taxi to the airport."

"What!?"

"If this pirate plot turns out to be part of a bigger conspiracy, we have to cover our tracks."

"And so, the rental agency loses a bunch of money?"

"Nah, they're insured. Some big national insurance company loses a bit, and they'll write it off their taxes."

"What about those people in the Mercedes? You almost killed them!"

"You mean those people shooting at us? I aimed for the engine block, and I only put one bullet in it to reduce the chance of it exploding."

"How charitable," Jana grumbled. "We should put you up for the Nobel Peace Prize."

"It was that or continue to be target practice."

"We wouldn't have been target practice if we hadn't stolen their map!"

"And who did that, you or me?"

Jana flushed, gripping the wheel tight. "You got an answer for everything, don't you? You're just like ..." Her words trailed off into an indistinct mumble.

"Just like who?"

"Nothing."

They drove in silence for a time. The sign for the highway came up. They never had managed to take a turnoff. That Mercedes had caught up with them too quickly.

"Don't get on it," Jacob warned. "They might search for us there, and if we come across a cop, they'll stop us for having no sideview mirrors. Take the access road instead."

Jana didn't reply but did as he suggested.

Jacob reached into the back seat, wiped a bunch of glass off the framed map, and picked it up. Sitting back down, he angled it so she could see.

"This looks pretty precise considering the time period. It shouldn't be too hard for a diver to find the wreck."

Silence.

"Might take a little time, of course, the spot won't be right on. No X marks the spot like in the old movies, eh?"

Silence. Jacob put on a grin. "Hey, aren't you excited about going after pirate treasure?"

"It's not treasure, you idiot, it's some live virus culture a group of thugs want to use as a bioweapon."

Jacob's grin didn't falter. "Even better. We'll be saving the world. Third time in as many months. Life sure got interesting lately, didn't it?"

"Oh yeah, real interesting! I get torn away from my excavation, get torn away from a guy I like, to commit felonies and get shot at. Yeah, Jacob, you're a thrill a minute!"

A guy she likes? Jacob felt a spike of jealousy. Trying to ignore that revelation, he said, "Sorry about your dig, but this is more important. I bet it feels more rewarding too."

"Did it ever occur to you that maybe I don't want to be caught up in all this? That maybe I'd rather have a normal, sane life? No, it didn't even cross your mind because you're an addict, Jacob. A damn adrenaline junkie just like Dad."

And so are you, Jacob thought. *Just like Dad.*

He didn't dare say that, though.

She's got the spark, Aaron Peters always used to say. *She's got the drive and the cool head. But she doesn't want this kind of life. She went for her own career, and I respect her for it.*

Did she know that? Did she know that Dad always spoke of her with a mixture of admiration and longing?

Yeah, Dad. He'd become like a dad to him. Jacob's real father had been a good man, a high school football coach who had inspired a whole generation of kids to excel and had brought home the state trophy several years running. Dad had been proud of his son when he went into the Rangers but had sadly died of cancer a year later. The whole town attended his funeral. Former students had flown in from half a dozen different states to attend.

Jacob hadn't. He'd been on a mission hunting Taliban.

And after his breakdown, after that dark period of insanity, Aaron Peters had plucked him out of Afghanistan and brought his soul back to life. He had become his second father.

One day, three years after that and after Jacob had been inducted into the CIA, he had asked Aaron if he could call him Dad.

Aaron had said yes with the formality of sealing a bond.

It was the only time he had seen Aaron Peters cry.

But Jacob could tell Jana none of these things. He had no idea how she would react, but he knew damn well it wouldn't be in a positive way.

Besides, he needed her help in catching these pirates.

And what would she say to that sort of thinking? More of the old "ends justify the means" crap she always hated from Dad. Just like the stunt we just pulled.

But what choice did he have? At the very least, they had a chance to intercept and neutralize a modern crew of pirates, no doubt saving lives in the future. At the very worst, they were stopping a bioweapon plot, in which case they were saving a whole lot more lives.

Either way, he needed to go to Venezuela, and he needed her help.

Yes, that kind of thinking was mercenary. It used other people to get the desired result. But it was necessary. Jana should understand that, did understand that at some level, but her resentment of her father—his second father—got in the way.

So, he stayed silent, getting on his phone, and finding a flight to Venezuela for the two of them. He'd pay for it out of one of his false identities, using the CIA slush fund. He'd get in trouble with Wallace for that, but if this turned out to be as big as Jacob suspected, the old warrior would forgive him.

The more important question was—would Jana Peters ever forgive him?

CHAPTER TEN

Fez, Morocco
That same day

Alpha One was seriously pissed, and that made Delta Two seriously nervous. As he tailed the American tourist through the labyrinthine alleyways of the old medina, Delta Two thought over all the things that had gone wrong.

The operation in the Khyber Pass had failed miserably. Delta Four, one of the best fighters The Order had available for field operations, had gone after Aaron Peters and had been taken out.

While fourth in ranking in The Order's hierarchy of combat operatives, Delta Four had been the most qualified for that particular operation. As a Kashmiri, Delta Four had far more experience than his superiors in mountain survival and combat. As a Muslim, he could blend into the towns and villages of that region.

After a year of painstaking recon ops, The Order had finally tracked Aaron Peters down and had sent the best man they had for the job.

That best man was now dead.

Even worse, Delta Two's own operation in Greece had failed.

They had narrowed down the location of Jacob Snow's residence to somewhere not far east of Athens, not that he ever spent much time there. The big break came when they had learned about his girlfriend Gabriella Cremonesi, a civilian who proved easy enough to manipulate. All they had to do was use one of The Order's shell companies to create an independent film company and then hire Cremonesi to make a film near Jacob Snow's house. Then Delta Two made a show of stalking her, knowing she'd call him for help.

After that, springing the trap was easy.

At least theoretically.

He had been ordered not to engage Jacob Snow directly.

"Too dangerous," Alpha One had said, "Even with a full team."

Delta Two and several of his team had disagreed but had been overruled. While Alpha One listened to the men and women under his command and considered their points of view, The Order was not a democracy.

So, Delta Two had set off a bomb. Once Jacob lay unconscious and helpless, he had come out of the bathroom where he had been hiding in order to finish him off.

And then the worst possible thing had happened—a police car had shown up.

Impossibly bad luck. The patrol car, rarely seen on that rural stretch of road, had just happened to be driving by when the bomb detonated. The police had immediately pulled into the taverna, and the two cops had jumped out, guns drawn, to investigate.

It was all Delta Two could do to get away without being seen.

Of course, he could have gunned down the cops easily enough, but that would have meant killing everyone else in the taverna as well. That would have been sloppy, very sloppy, and The Order did not like sloppy.

So, Delta Two had fled the scene, hoping Jacob Snow was already dead.

Now the intel said he wasn't dead. Unfortunately, none of the operatives in that sector had any idea where he was.

The best guess was the U.S. military hospital in Crete, but there was no way they were getting in there. Or he might have been released already. If that was the case, then there was no telling where he might have gone.

The only way to find out was to track down one of his weak points—the civilians he had befriended.

Using Gabriella Cremonesi had almost worked. Maybe a second try with Jana Peters would work better.

Except she had vanished too.

So here he was, following Brian Tanner while a local guide showed Brian the medieval medina of Fez, one of Morocco's historic cities.

Luckily, Fez was popular with tourists, and the guide, an old man in a brown djellaba and white turban, was showing Brian all the main sights. That made it easy enough for Delta Two to walk at a discrete distance, taking all the usual photos people took. He had followed Brian and the guide down the main street of the souk lined with shops and stalls, the crowd thick and the air heavy with the smells of cooking and incense. They stopped to admire the outsides of a couple of old mosques and madrasas. Brian, not being Muslim, was not allowed in and contented himself with taking pictures of the ornate gates and minarets. Delta Two took some pictures, too, and got close enough to overhear the archaeology graduate student mention he was staying in an Airbnb. Good. The privacy would make it easier to grab him.

Then the guide led him down a narrower but still busy street, through shaded courtyards to admire splashing fountains decorated in blue and green tile, before taking him on a tour of the tannery.

Delta Two stayed outside for that one. The tannery of Fez was a huge place that stank so badly that visitors were given a sprig of mint to hold under their nose, so they didn't faint. Delta Two had been in there before and didn't want to repeat the experience. Besides, there was only one way in and out.

Brain came out half an hour later, looking a bit green around the gills, and the guide took him back to the market for some tea and Moroccan sweets. Delta Two positioned himself in a different café across the street and watched him until the guide took him uphill toward the upper medina. Delta Two followed.

As the crowd grew thicker, Delta Two got closer to his quarry, and overheard snippets of conversation.

"… a great tour … wish I had more mint ha ha … think I'll take a nap before exploring more of the town … great view from the roof …"

"Here you go, sir," the old guide said, stopping at a door.

"Thanks. I've been in Morocco a few months now, and it's still hard getting around your old cities."

"You are welcome anytime, my friend."

Delta Two passed by, not looking at them. He rounded a corner, stepped into a doorway, and got on his phone.

He texted "about to pick up some groceries" to his backup team, who had been trailing him while keeping out of sight of the target as much as possible. Delta Two would go in alone to subdue and question Brian while his backup team would keep watch. It shouldn't take long. The guy was a civvie. He'd break easily enough.

The old guide passed by, not even sparing him a glance. Delta Two waited until he disappeared beyond another corner and went back to Brain's place.

It was a simple, wooden door among many along this alley. Each would lead to a house or a series of private levels with a common stairway.

Delta Two gave a quick glance in either direction to make sure no one was watching, then scanned the rooftops. You don't get much privacy in a Moroccan medina. Women and girls often peeked from windows and rooftops. He didn't see any at the moment, and they were unlikely to interfere in a foreigner's business anyway.

He slipped a set of lockpicks out of his pocket and got the lock open in less than five seconds. Just then, a pair of Moroccan men came around the corner, speaking in low tones to one another, their faces half hidden by the hoods of their heavy cloaks of brown wool. Delta Two shifted his body to shield his hands from view, so the pair would assume he was simply using a key.

He palmed his lockpick into his sleeve, passed through the door, and closed it quietly behind him.

A staircase, dimly lit by a single screened window at the next landing, ran up. A door stood to his left, as did another on the landing above and a third at the top landing.

Delta Two headed for the top floor, remembering Brain's remark about a rooftop view.

As he passed the middle landing, he heard the sounds of Arabic conversation within. He'd have to be extra careful. Alpha One had picked him not only for his deadliness but also for his stealth. He could handle someone like Brian Tanner with no problems.

He got to the top landing and could see bright daylight filtering in from beneath the wooden door. That meant a split-level roof, common enough in this country. Brian's place was an addition onto a previously existing roof, probably taking up one half of the area with an airshaft at the center of the roof providing light to the lower stories.

Damn. That meant the neighbors would hear everything. He had to take care.

Delta Two opened the lock in a few seconds and walked in casually. As he expected, he saw a large, square rooftop space, an airshaft in the middle surrounded by a railing, and to one side, an addition that had been converted into an Airbnb. A flight of steps went up the side to a higher rooftop, shaded by a tarpaulin. In the other three directions, the square rooftops of Fez spread out before him like a checkerboard.

Just as Delta Two closed the door behind him, Brian walked out of the addition. He stopped and blinked.

"Um, hello," he said uncertainly.

Delta Two feigned surprise. "Oh, are you the guy who rented this before me?"

"What? No, I'm renting it right now. I have it for three more days."

Delta Two rolled his eyes and groaned. "Ugh, not again! Airbnbs in Morocco always mess up the dates."

He closed the distance between them. Brian's face registered the first hint of suspicion.

"All that's done via the website. And how did you get in here?"

Delta Two glanced down the airshaft. No sign of the downstairs neighbors, although he could hear them talking down there.

"I came in with my key, the one they gave me. What's the Wi-Fi code? I'll send an email to the host."

Brian hesitated a moment then said, "Hold on, it's on the bottom of the router."

The archaeologist turned to walk back into the addition. Delta Two gave him a quick karate chop to the neck, and Brian fell hard to the floor without so much as a cry. Delta Two dragged him inside, closed the door behind him, and took a quick look around. It was a bedroom area opening into a kitchenette and a tiny bathroom.

"Went for the cheap option, I see," Delta Two muttered, pulling out a zip tie and securing Brian's hands behind his back. "But hey, after living in a tent for the past three months, this must seem luxurious."

Brian groaned and shifted. Delta Two hauled him onto the bed and pulled out a broad, razor-sharp knife. He clamped a hand over Brian's mouth. The archaeologist's eyes went wide.

"I can kill you silently," Delta Two said, "and I can torture you just as silently. I can make you suffer. I can take body parts. I can leave you a hideous mess, or I can take your life. Or, and this is something you should consider, I can let you go unharmed. Now, I'm going to take my hand away, and if you scream or talk above a whisper, I'll kill you instantly. Understand?"

Brian nodded, eyes bugged with terror. Delta Two let his hand go, keeping the point of his knife hovering over his prisoner's left eye.

"I … I don't have much money on me," he whispered.

Delta Two snorted. "Don't be stupid. You think that's what I'm here for?"

Brian paled. "Oh, wait. It's got something to do with Jana, doesn't it?"

Delta Two nodded. "Where is she?"

"I … I don't understand. You tried killing her, didn't you? The cops fobbed that off as a random terrorist attack, but that's not true, is it? And those trips she took away, she said it was a sick relative, but I always suspected she was lying. She's involved in something, isn't she? What is it? You're a criminal gang? You making her smuggle drugs or something?"

Delta Two stopped his babbling with a quick slap.

"Who I am and what I represent is no concern of yours. You should be thinking about your own safety. Tell me where she is."

Brian blinked. "I don't know."

"What do you mean, you don't know?"

"She said she was flying back to the States, to her university, but she left two days early, so I think she's made another one of her random disappearances."

"And where does she disappear to?"

"I don't know."

Delta Two lowered the knife so that the tip lightly touched his eyeball. Brain pressed his head into the mattress, screwing his eyes shut.

"You're her assistant. Judging from the way you two interact, you got the hots for her. You're asking me to believe she hasn't told you anything?"

"She hasn't. I swear!"

"Keep your voice down. I won't tell you again."

Delta Two was inclined to believe him. He could generally tell when a prisoner was lying or not. Well, after a bit of cutting he'd see. He pulled a gag out of his back pocket.

Just then his phone buzzed. He'd set it up only to do that if he got an urgent message from his backup team.

He yanked out his phone. The message contained one word.

"Intercepted."

Delta Two swore. He rushed out onto the rooftop just in time to hear the downstairs door bang open.

He opened the door to the staircase and saw three burly strangers, all Moroccan, swarm up the staircase, MP5 submachine guns in hand.

Delta Two threw his knife at them and ducked back so fast he didn't even see if he hit. He sprinted across the roof, leapt onto the low surrounding wall, and took a long jump over the intervening alley to the other rooftop.

He just made it, tucking into a roll that stopped abruptly as he came up hard against a wooden bench.

That didn't stop him for long. He got to his feet, sprinted across the roof, and leapt to the next one.

A Moroccan woman hanging laundry there let out a yell. Delta Two ran right past her, angling to put her in between himself and his pursuers.

"Get down!" a man shouted behind him in Arabic.

The shocked woman didn't respond, giving Delta Two cover long enough to leap to the next rooftop.

This alley was wider, however, and Delta Two realized as he sailed through the air that he wouldn't make it. He reached out and clamped onto the lip of the wall with his hands. For a sickening moment, he thought his grasp would slip, but he just managed to hold on.

He looked below him. A wide alley yawned at his dangling feet, two stories of empty air before a surface of hard flagstones.

But there, just to his right and one story down, was a little sloped tile roof for a window, built to provide shade for the couple of hours when the hard Moroccan sun glared down on it.

Would it hold his weight? He doubted it. He did a pull up, then ducked back down as a burst of gunfire raked the rooftop.

Damn, those guys had hopped across the rooftops too? Those weren't cops; they were commandoes. Looked like Jana had friends in high places.

He edged along the lip of the wall until he got above the window, then let go as another burst chewed up the plaster where his fingers had been a moment before.

Delta Two fell, impacted the little roof, which cracked but did not shatter, and he hung from it for a second before dropping down.

A long freefall. He landed harder than he wanted to, rolled to reduce the force, and came up running. Limping, but running. A burst of bullets stitched a line in the flagstones after him before he got around the corner and away.

That civilian would survive, but Jana Peters had just become The Order's top priority. If the Moroccan secret service was protecting her, that meant she was working with Jacob Snow.

And that meant they needed to get her. Get her, and they'd get Aaron Peters, and they'd get Jacob Snow as well.

The Order's two biggest threats taken out in one blow.

All they needed to do was get that woman.

71

CHAPTER ELEVEN

Caracas, Venezuela
The next afternoon

Jacob yawned, rubbed his eyes, and resisted the urge to slap the local CIA field office director.

Arnold Reece wore a jacket and tie and sat behind an immaculate desk, looking for all the world like a middle-aged, middle manager in some large corporate office hellhole. Jacob knew Reece was an expert on Latin America and had done his time as a field agent, but he didn't look like it, and he sure didn't act like it.

"I'm sorry, Agent Snow, but I'm afraid I can't equip you if you're on vacation. This wild goose chase that you're on isn't CIA work. In fact, you shouldn't be doing it at all."

"There's a clear and present danger."

"From a ship that sank 250 years ago? Come on."

They'd been through this before, round and round for the past quarter hour. Jacob had declined to inform him that he'd brought Jana along. Currently, she was buried in the national archives, trying to find out more about the *Nueva Esperanza*, Doctor Sebastián de Ulloa, the Black Fever, the *Santo Santiago*, and the *Vengeance*.

That was her job. His job was to gear up in the local CIA station's armory, and he was failing at that job.

"Look, I've been on missions following a lot thinner and more unlikely trails than this. I can't talk about them but—"

"You're not on a mission, Agent Snow. You're supposed to be back in the European sector monitoring communications. We have a very delicate political situation here in Venezuela. The country is bankrupt, the populace is angry, and there are whispers of an impending revolution. We can't have you gallivanting around the countryside looking for pirate treasure."

Jacob growled with frustration. He didn't know what "gallivanting" meant, but he was pretty sure it meant that he wouldn't get to do what he wanted. He hated it when people kept him from doing what he wanted, since their reasons for doing so were almost always wrong.

Station Director Reece's face remained impassive. Jacob could tell he wasn't going to get anywhere, and if he pushed it, he might just find himself in custody.

There was a knock on the door.

"Come in," Reece called in a tone that made it plain their business was over.

A female agent came in and handed Reece a note. The agent withdrew, closing the door behind her. Reece read the note, gave Jacob a sharp look, and asked, "Do you have a civilian named Jana Peters here with you?"

Oh, crap. You've done your homework.

"She came here of her own free will."

Reece frowned. "I didn't ask if you kidnapped her, Agent Snow, I asked if she was with you. I guess the answer is yes. Where is she at the moment?"

"The National Archives."

"Equip yourself in the armory and collect her immediately. Then bring her back here."

Jacob blinked. "I beg your pardon?"

"You heard me. Make sure you aren't followed. Once you get back, both you and her have a phone call to make."

***

An hour later, Jacob and a rather bewildered Jana sat in an isolation room in the CIA field office. An isolation room is a specially constructed space in the interior of an embassy or field office that it is impenetrable to any remote listening devices. The only communication in or out, besides the door, is via a coded satellite uplink.

Before them stood a computer going through an encrypted program to bring up the caller.

When the screen lit up, Jacob jerked with surprise. He had expected Tyler Wallace, instead he got Farid Jalloul.

A narrow-faced Moroccan man of indeterminate age, Farid was an undercover agent for the Moroccan counterterrorism service. He had been on a couple of jobs with Jacob, most recently tracking down Karim ibn Mohammed, dubbed the "Master of Pain" for the many Dark Web videos he posted of himself torturing so-called "enemies of Islam."

The Master of Pain was now enduring some pain of his own in some dark cell somewhere.

Farid served under General Jaloul Cherkaoui, commander of the Moroccan counterterrorism service, working out of an ultra-secret base in the medina of Marrakech. A good man working for a great one.

"Hello, Farid, what's up?" Jacob said in Arabic. *Nothing good, obviously.*

"Hello, my friend, and hello Ms. Peters," Farid replied in the same language. "Whoever is behind the attempt on your life has tried again, this time by trying to kidnap Brian Tanner."

"Brian!" Jana cried. "Is he all right?"

Again, Jacob felt a little spike of jealousy.

"He is fine, Ms. Peters. He is currently in one of our safehouses. When you left, we decided to track him because we know the two of you are close. Forgive me, but we observed you at the seaside restaurant in Asilah."

Jacob squirmed in his seat.

"You were spying on us?" Jana said.

"Watching over you, Ms. Peters. When your archaeological field crew dispersed, we suspected that if there would be a move against any of them, it would be against Mr. Tanner. He rented an apartment in Fez, and we put it under surveillance. On the afternoon of his first day there, a foreign man, most likely American, broke into his place and threatened to kill him if he didn't reveal where you were."

"Oh my God," Jana groaned, putting her face in her hands.

"We intervened before he was hurt. The attacker got away, I'm afraid, as did his backup team, who all appeared to be Moroccan nationals familiar with Fez. They must have had a safehouse they retreated to. We're currently searching for them."

They evaded Farid? Jacob thought with wonder. *Damn, these guys are good.*

"Did this Brian guy give a description of his attacker?" Jacob asked.

"Yes, and we did a composite sketch. I'll put it onscreen."

Farid's face was replaced with a drawing of a square-jawed, bulky man with a crew cut.

"Recognize him?" Jacob asked.

"No," Jana replied.

"Neither do I."

"Mr. Tanner says he spoke with an American accent with no strong regional flavor. He thinks he might be from the northern or northern midwestern states, or the West Coast. The attacker revealed nothing about himself, only that he wanted to know the location of Ms. Peters."

"Do you have any other details about him? Any other details at all?"

"Very good at picking locks. His knife throwing ability was good as well. Thankfully our lead man was wearing Kevlar. Very fit. Led us on a merry chase across the rooftops of Fez. Other than that, no, we have nothing."

"Who could this guy be working for?" Jacob said.

"Your guess is as good as mine, my friend. He didn't strike me as a jihadist, but one can never tell these days. The West is spitting up the most unlikely recruits."

"Tell me about it," Jacob grumbled. On his last mission, he had taken out a couple of those recruits, young American kids who should have been back home chasing girls and taking college classes. Instead, they were living in the middle of the Sahara toting automatic weapons.

"Well, Jana is safe for the moment. They won't be able to track us here."

"She used her passport to fly to Caracas, didn't she?" Farid asked.

"Yeah, but we're about to go off-grid, assuming the local station chief lets us."

"Good. I'll keep you informed. And Ms. Peters, don't worry about your boyfriend. We will protect him and get him out of the country safely. We will also keep him in the dark. He thinks that a terrorist group wants to kill you because you uncovered a pagan mosaic. Let him continue to think that. The less he knows, the better."

"I don't think they'll target him now that they know he knows nothing, and that you're watching," Jacob said.

"God, let's hope so," Jana muttered.

"We'll keep vigilant in any case," Farid said. "I'll send you updates if I get any. Goodbye for now."

The screen went dark.

Jacob stared at it for a moment, not wanting to face Jana.

When he finally turned to her, he saw just what he expected to see—an angry look.

"Sorry," he mumbled. Not that it was his fault, really.

"It's bad enough you've roped me into your world, but Brian? He has no training, no preparation for this."

75

Jacob took a deep breath. "I contacted you because it was necessary. I needed your help with the Suez Canal bomb. I couldn't have solved it without you. Thousands, maybe millions would have died. I needed your help in Jerusalem too."

He didn't mention that their partial failure in that mission had led to rioting across the Middle East. Thousands had probably died from that. She already knew that. Although millions more would have died if they hadn't intervened. She knew that too.

There was a long, awkward silence. It got broken by a rapping on the door.

"Come in," Jacob called.

Director Reece entered, looking irritated. "I just spoke with your superior in Athens. I've been told to give you every assistance I can."

Jacob perked up. "Good. There are a few more things I need from the armory."

"Take what you want."

"Can I get a couple of field agents? Preferably with boating and diving experience?"

"I don't have any field agents to spare, not with all that's going on."

"But I need backup! We're going after a whole pirate crew."

"Who may or may not even be there. I have a potential revolution to deal with. Wallace said to help you, not mollycoddle you."

Jacob didn't know what "mollycoddle" meant, but he took it to mean he wasn't getting any more help from Reece than some gear.

"Never mind," Jacob grumbled. "I'll deal with that end myself."

Reece turned to Jana. "Ms. Peters, I can get you on the next plane back to the United States. I can spare a field agent to escort you to the airport."

"The airport? I'm not going anywhere."

Reece blinked. "You're staying here?"

Jacob grinned. "Because of my irresistible personality."

He instantly regretted his joke when she glowered at him. "No, I'm staying because you can't do it alone."

"And we can't do it with just the two of us. But don't worry, I got some help I can call on."

"Help? What kind of help?"

Jacob gave her a sheepish grin. "A guy I know. He can be a little …abrasive."

Jana put her hands on her hips. "More abrasive than you?"

Reece let out a little titter.

Jacob ignored him and replied, "More abrasive than me? Oh, Jana, you have no idea."

CHAPTER TWELVE

The Venezuelan coast
midnight

Jana looked around nervously at the abandoned beach, all but pitch black under an overcast sky. The sea was nothing more than a vague, whitish movement of breakers in the gloom accompanied by a constant *shush shush* of the waves as they hit the unseen sand.

Jacob walked ahead, a shadow against the darkness, moving with a purpose and confidence that showed he had been here many times before.

She wished she knew where "here" was. They had driven a CIA vehicle to the parking lot of a rural hostel, left it there, and then struck out half a mile to get to the beach. Then they had walked along the tree line next to the dunes for at least a couple of miles, stumbling over roots, once hunkering down and circling inland to avoid a group of teenagers who had built a bonfire on the beach. The strumming of their guitar and innocent laughter followed them for some time.

Then, at a dark spot that looked no different than any of the others, Jacob had abruptly turned toward the sand. They had gone over dunes and were now on the level part of the beach. He seemed determined to walk straight into the surf.

Jana followed. She didn't trust this man to tell her the truth about her father, she didn't trust him to obey the law, but she did trust him not to steer her wrong.

A sudden thumping just ahead made her jerk and go for the gun hidden below her windbreaker. A moment later, she eased up. She found herself walking on wooden boards, the sound of her footfalls making a thumping with each step.

They were on a pier, a pier she couldn't see until she was actually walking on it.

How the hell had he found this place?

A sharp, low whistle from somewhere up ahead made them both stop. Jacob said something in German. Jana knew a bit of the language but didn't catch what he said. A male voice said something back, again in German. The guy sounded drunk.

There followed a quick back and forth in German. Jana could pick out just enough to tell that Jacob was identifying himself and saying a few nonsense phrases that were obviously code words.

"Here," the male voice said, switching to Spanish. A pinpoint of light appeared, illuminating a small portion of a boat's hull next to the pier. Jacob stepped on first. Before Jana could follow, the light swung up to shine in her eyes. She stopped, holding her hand up, blinking.

"Is she all right?" the voice asked, still in Spanish. Jana thought she detected an Argentinian accent.

"You think I'd bring her if she wasn't?" Jacob said.

"Does she speak Spanish?"

"And Arabic, and probably a few other languages I don't know about."

"You should know everything about her."

"Um, I'm right here," Jana said. She hated being talked about in her presence.

"Yeah, you are. Nice accent. You learned in Mexico like all the other Americans," the male voice said.

"Not Jacob," Jana pointed out. "He speaks with a Salvadoran accent."

"Don't pry into people's past," the male voice said.

"Don't be such a dork," a young female voice said from somewhere further off. It sounded like a teenager.

"If I'm a dork, I'm the coolest dork you've ever met," the male voice replied.

"What. Ever."

Yes, definitely a teenager.

"You get seasick?" the male voice asked.

"No," Jana replied.

"Do you know how to scuba dive?"

"I'm not an expert, but yes."

"Are you a Jew?"

"I beg your pardon?"

"You heard me. Are you a Jew?"

"No. You got something against Jews?"

"It's going to be five grand, Jacob. Ten if we take fire."

"All right," Jacob said.

"Wait. Why are you asking me if I'm a Jew?" Jana asked.

79

"Get in the boat," the Argentinian ordered.

The light swung back down to show her the way. She stepped in.

The light switched off. The boat rocked slightly as someone moved around. The teenage girl spoke again.

"Walk right toward me and you'll be fine. I'll lead you down decks."

She spoke Spanish with a Venezuelan accent.

Jana shuffled forward, completely blinded by the afterimages in her eyes, reaching out with her hands.

A pair of slim female hands, surprisingly calloused, grabbed her.

"OK. Duck your head and feel with your feet. We're coming to some stairs," the girl said.

Jana crouched low and cautiously probed in the darkness to find the steps. The girl led her down them and steered her through the cabin. Jana bumped her hip against something she presumed to be a table before the girl set her down on a padded bench.

"Just stay there. I have to go back on deck and help Dad with the sails."

"We're sailing?"

"We can't risk the noise of the engine. We'll turn that on later."

Then she was gone. Jana sat in darkness, listening to the soft footsteps on deck, then the snap of a sail being unfurled.

Sitting there alone in the dark, Jana wondered at the strange turn her life had taken. This was the third time she'd been pulled out of her research to help deal with a threat of potentially global implications. Would it happen again? Would her life keep getting interrupted by terrorists? Even if it didn't, could she ever live a normal life knowing what she knew and having seen what she'd seen?

She wondered if her father ever sat in the dark, feeling that same surreal disconnect with the regular world, and knowing that duty forced him to move forward with the mission.

There was the thud of what she assumed was the mooring rope being taken in and then she felt the boat move.

Right after that, Jana heard another sound, a low scuttling across the floor.

She stiffened. Had that been a rat?

The scuttling came closer. She strained her eyes and ears but couldn't make anything out.

Then something sleek and furry brushed her bare arm. She let out a cry.

"Keep your voice down!" the male voice hissed from on deck.

"There are rats down here," Jana said, moving away from what had touched her, only to bang up against a bulkhead.

"That's not a rat," the girl said. "That's Davey Jones."

"Huh?"

"My ferret."

"You have a ferret?"

"Don't worry, it doesn't bite."

"Much," her father added.

Jana sat, hoping Davey Jones didn't decide to get friendly. The boat felt like it was picking up speed.

Someone came down below.

"Who's that?"

"Ahoy maties!" Jacob said. "We be hunting the treasure of—" THUD "—ow!"

"Jacob, you are such a klutz," the girl said from somewhere above them.

"You know Jacob?" Jana asked.

"Sure. He's almost as much of a dork as my dad."

"Kid, I think we're going to get along just fine," Jana said.

They continued to sail into the darkness. The strange father and daughter remained busy on deck, and Jacob started snoring. Jana sat where she was, occasionally feeling Davey Jones's whiskers as he gave her a sniff. Despite her jetlag and weariness, Jana couldn't sleep, not in circumstances like this.

Although she knew she should. She had a feeling she'd need all the strength she had for the work to come.

***

They sailed in silence for another two hours before the captain flicked on the lights. Jana blinked at the sudden brightness and found herself in the main cabin of a large boat. Jacob lay asleep on a nearby bench, a ferret curled up on his chest, studying Jana with beady, black eyes.

She went up on deck to find the crew furling the sail, which was made of canvas dyed black. The captain was a light-skinned man in his early forties, his hair beginning to go gray under his sailor's cap. His daughter, a slim girl of about fourteen, was much darker, with raven black hair, brown skin, and eyes such a deep brown as to almost be black.

"Hi," the girl chirped. "Welcome to the *Searunner*. I'm Eva. My dad's name is Néstor."

"Um, hi."

"We'll get the engine started in a minute," Néstor said. "You got that map Jacob told me about?"

"Yeah. I'll fetch it."

Eva followed her below decks, where Jana had left her bag.

"You from the United States?" the girl asked.

"Yeah."

"We sailed all the way to New York once. We saw *The Lion King* on Broadway."

"Your dad sail to other countries a lot?" Jana asked, pulling out the folder where she kept the old map.

"All the time. We're at sea most of the year."

"Don't you go to school?"

"I learn more out here. Miss my friends, though. Wow! Cool map."

Néstor walked through the cabin. "Come on through to the helm and we'll plot a course."

Jacob let out a yawn. Davey Jones the ferret hopped off his chest, scampered over to Eva, and scrabbled up her to sit on her shoulder.

"Hey, baby," Eva said, scratching the animal behind its ear.

Jana followed the captain through a small doorway to the helm. Jana didn't know much about boats, but the instruments all looked new and expensive. There was enough room for two seats, a small space behind them, and an access door on one side to the deck. She sat in the seat next to the captain's.

"We might encounter pirates, you know," Jana said, casting a concerned look through the doorway at the teenager cooing over her pet. "It's not safe for her to be here."

"Safer than on land. There's probably going to be a revolution later this week. After this job, I'm thinking of taking a nice vacation in Belize until things calm down. Eva likes the beaches there."

"Where's her mother?"

Néstor's face fell. "Dead," he said. "In another revolution."

"Sorry. I didn't mean to pry."

"Full-blooded Indian from Nicaragua. Good thing Eva got her looks and my sailing ability and not the other way around. My wife never liked the sea. It was the only thing we didn't agree on."

"I'm sorry," Jana said again, resolving not to ask this obviously private man any more questions.

She broke that promise a moment later when she saw what was dangling from the ship's wheel.

"What the hell is that?" she demanded, pointing, and already knowing the answer.

"An Iron Cross. World War Two German medal."

"What's it doing hanging from your ship's wheel?"

"It was my grandfather's. He was a *Sturmbannführer* in the *SS Totenkopfverbände*. The Death's Head Division. That was the division responsible for overseeing the concentration camps. He fled to Argentina after the war. That's why I have such light skin and blue eyes."

Jana went cold. "You're a …"

"A Nazi?" Néstor gave her an amused look. "Of course not. If I lived back then, I would have been arrested for miscegenation and Eva would have been sent to the camps."

"Then why keep that awful thing?"

"To remind myself, and my daughter, that evil can hide behind friendly faces. Grandpa was always so nice to me. Taught me German, fed me ice cream, took me to the amusement park. A great guy, until I learned the truth."

"Wait. Why did you ask if I was Jewish?"

Néstor shot her a grin. "Because if you were, the ride would have been free. Show me that map and let's plot a course."

Jana showed him the map. He let out a whistle. Eva entered the cabin, and Jacob stood in the doorway.

"A real treasure map," Néstor said. "Never thought I'd see one of those."

"Cooool," Eva said, leaning over his shoulder to look. Davey Jones, wrapped around her neck, looked too.

"That location is pretty precise," the captain said. "I can get us there a little after dawn. You sure this map is accurate, though? I've heard a lot of treasure maps are fake."

"This one isn't," Jana reassured him. As she said it, she realized something—why would someone make a map that correctly pointed out the location of a sunken pirate ship? Wouldn't they put the location in code or something? It didn't make any sense.

She held up the map to the light. The paper was mottled and stained from age. She sniffed it, but she smelled nothing except a bit of mustiness.

"What are you doing?" Jacob asked.

"Anyone got a lighter?"

"My dad does. He smokes these really stinky Cuban cigars."

Néstor produced a lighter.

Jana flicked it on and brought it behind the map.

"What are you doing?" Jacob cried.

"Relax."

She brought the lighter closer behind the old paper, running it back and forth to warm the entire surface while taking care not to burn it.

As she did, faint, brown lines began to appear, a different set of triangulation lines than those written in ink.

"Whoa," Eva said. "Invisible ink."

"They must have written that with lemon juice," Jacob said.

"Or any acidic liquid," Jana said. "Given the period, most likely they used urine."

"Eeew," Jacob said. "How do you even know that?"

Jana smiled. "You pick up a lot of odd information when you go to archaeology conferences."

"Well, you didn't have to share it," Jacob said.

"I agree with Jacob," Eva said. "That's seriously gross."

Néstor leaned over and sniffed. "Ah! The sweet smell of pirate pee."

"You're such a dork, Dad."

Jana peered at it. "It shows a different location for the wreck, not far off from the one marked on the map."

"Why didn't the mapmaker put the ink spot somewhere completely different?" Néstor asked.

"Because the general location was in the records, he couldn't steer the reader too far wrong without arousing suspicion."

"Huh. Well, I'll change the course."

Jacob smiled. "Clever trick. But even better, I bet the copies don't have that invisible ink."

Jana smiled back. "I bet they don't."

"We'll get there a little after dawn," Néstor announced. "I prefer to pilot the ship alone, so all of you get out of my cabin."

The captain let out a loud fart.

"Augh! Dad, you are so embarrassing!"

A terrible stench filled the cabin. They all fled onto the deck for some fresh air.

"I told you he was more annoying than I am," Jacob said.

"I didn't believe you at first, but now I do," Jana replied.

Jana walked to the prow of the ship, holding onto the guardrail to steady herself in the gentle swell.

Eva came up to her. "Sorry about my dad. He's a loser."

"Be glad you have him. I grew up without a dad. I'd have preferred an annoying dad over an absent one."

Out of the corner of her eye, she saw Jacob turn away.

"Damn. That sucks," Eva said. She peered out into the darkness. "You really think there's a pirate ship out there somewhere?"

"Yeah. Somewhere out there lies the wreck of the *Santo Santiago*."

"You think there's gold on it? Diamonds?"

"Maybe."

Or more likely, something that could kill us all.

CHAPTER THIRTEEN

The sun peeked over the horizon, making it look like a road paved with gold ran from it to the sailboat. Jacob stood on deck, breathing in the fresh air of the Caribbean, and feeling miserable. Being at sea made him think of Gabriella. She loved sailing, and a few times he'd taken out his sailboat and they had spent days plying the routes through the Greek islands, swimming in the clear water, and making love on deck under the stars.

Making love? No. Just having sex. Jacob couldn't recall if he had ever made love. Doing the job he did, he had to keep an emotional distance between himself and the few unknowing civilians in his life. It was necessary, both for himself and for them.

Not that it had protected Gabriella. Damn, such a beautiful, kind, talented woman cut off in her late twenties by some bastard with a bomb.

He hadn't heard any updates from Wallace, which meant the investigation hadn't tracked down those responsible. He cursed his boss for not letting him join in the manhunt, while at the same time understanding why. He'd have gone in guns blazing and would have probably made all sorts of mistakes. You needed a cool head for an operation, and he couldn't manage that.

At least he had another operation. That made him feel better. Sort of.

But nothing could bring Gabriella back to life.

The sound of footsteps on deck made him turn. Néstor walked toward him with the wide, rolling gait of a sailor, a coffee cup in each hand.

"Thought you might like this," the Argentinian said.

"Thanks. Is Eva at the helm?"

"Yep. Getting to be as good as me."

"She was pretty good the last time we sailed together."

That had been two years before, when the kid had only been twelve. It was the only other time Jacob had to do a mission in the Caribbean, when he was tracking down a terror cell trying to infiltrate the U.S. by sea. Jacob had hired Néstor to get him from Cuba to Haiti no questions asked. It turned out a little more complicated than that. Somehow, Néstor had forgiven him.

"I'll teach her everything I know," the sailor said, "and then sit back and watch as she gets better than I ever was."

Jacob took a sip of his coffee. A rich, smooth brew from the Jinotega region of Nicaragua, in honor of a wife now gone.

"We'll get there in about an hour," Néstor said.

"Is Jana still asleep?"

"Yeah. Nice woman you got there. You and her having a thing?"

"No."

"Hmmm."

Jacob elbowed him.

"I'm not sure Eva would approve if you started catting around with a passenger."

Néstor chuckled. "She's the boss, that's for sure. But I can't live as a monk, can I? I shouldn't have farted. That might have ruined my chances."

"You don't have any chances."

The captain grinned. "Oooh. Jealous, are we?"

"No."

"Hmmm. You're usually a good liar. Don't worry, I don't think Jana likes me anyway, and I don't think she's over the shock of seeing that Iron Cross."

"You explained it, right?"

"Yeah, but she still thinks I'm weird."

"You are weird."

Néstor rolled his eyes and in a mock teenage voice said, "I am. So. Embarrassing."

The two men laughed. Under his mirth, Jacob felt a deep sadness. "You're lucky, you know," he said softly.

Néstor nodded. "I am."

The captain scanned the horizon with expert eyes. Jacob followed his gaze. The sea was fairly calm, the sky clear but for a few clouds. Jacob knew enough to know that boded well for the day's weather. No islands were in sight, although far to the northeast they could just make out a freighter close to the horizon.

They continued their circuit and saw a large fishing trawler far off to the west. It seemed to be going in the same direction as they were.

Jacob watched it for a time. He noticed Néstor watching it too.

"Looks like it's going to intercept us," the sailor said.

"Have they tried hailing us on the radio?" Jacob asked, cocking his ear. He could just hear the background crackle of the marine radio through an open porthole in the cabin.

"Eva would have told me."

"Got a pair of binoculars?" The boat was moving pretty fast for a fishing vessel. It had already closed a fifth of the distance.

"Sure."

Néstor hurried down below and returned a moment later with a pair of powerful binoculars.

He studied the vessel for a moment, then handed over the binoculars to Jacob.

Looking through them, he saw a mid-sized fishing boat with a powerful engine churning up the water behind it. The low roar of the motor came to him from across the water. He saw a couple of figures by the prow but couldn't make out any more from this distance.

"What do you think?" Jacob asked.

"They're definitely on an intercept course. Doesn't look like we can outrun them either."

"I don't see any weapons."

"Neither do I," Néstor said. "I'm getting my rifle just in case. I'll wake up Jana while I'm at it."

"Good idea. Get me my weapons bag. It's the—"

"Blue and white duffel bag? Yeah, I know."

The captain disappeared down below.

Jacob continued to watch the boat. The rational side of him said that it couldn't be the pirates, because how would they know the *Searunner* was anything more than the pleasure boat it appeared to be? The CIA side of him noted its general vector toward the spot shown on the map—the false spot, that is—and the fact that its engines had far more power than a fishing trawler needed.

Néstor came above decks, toting a high-powered rifle with a scope and Jacob's bag. He walked slumped, carrying the weapons below the line of the gunwale so the sailors on the other ship couldn't spot them.

The captain dropped the bag down at Jacob's feet with a clank. Jacob ducked down, unzipped it, and pulled out an MP5, wishing he had brought along a rifle too. He hadn't thought he'd need it. Most of the time, he fought in close quarters.

The fishing trawler cut its speed and pulled alongside, matching the *Searunner's* speed and direction about a hundred yards off its starboard side.

Jacob took a closer look through the binoculars. He could still see only three men on deck, far fewer than a boat like that would normally carry.

A couple of them looked to be of Mediterranean extraction. The third looked east African.

One of the Mediterranean guys cupped his hands around his mouth and shouted in Spanish, "Hello! Our radio and GPS have both broken. Can you give us a reading?"

Jacob stiffened. "That's the pirate captain," he said, keeping his voice low even though there was no chance they could hear. "The one I told you about."

"You sure?"

"Yeah. I recognize his voice and accent."

"Damn," Néstor muttered. "I got to get Eva in the tub."

The "tub" was a protective casing of titanium roughly the size and shape of a bathtub, stripped from an A-10 cockpit. Néstor had placed it below the bunks as a safe space for his daughter in case they took fire, which wasn't unknown in their lifestyle. How Néstor got his hands on it was something Jacob would probably never know.

Néstor cupped his hands and shouted back. "Cut your engines and so will I. I got her on cruise control."

"All right!" the pirate captain shouted back.

Jacob continued to scrutinize him through the binoculars. He looked like he might be Berber. Was that a Berber accent he was hearing? Might be, but a light one. If he really was Berber, he had spent a lot of time in Spain. He had the soft intonation of an Iberian, rather than the harder accent of a Latin American.

Néstor moved forward and entered the pilot's cabin. A few seconds later, the engines switched to idle and the *Searunner* began to slow. The fishing trawler did the same.

Then Néstor came back on deck. Right behind him came Jana, an M16 strapped to her back. She crawled along the deck to the stern and remained out of sight behind the gunwale.

"Eva safe?" Jacob asked.

"Safe as she can be. Let's keep her that way," Néstor said.

"What are you doing out here?" the pirate captain called over.

"Oh, just out for a pleasure cruise. Going to do some deep-sea fishing," Néstor replied.

"You're pretty far out for that."

"Oh, I got this gringo client. They can be pretty picky."

"Most of the pleasure boats stick closer to the shore."

Néstor faked a laugh. "Yeah, well, how can you explain that to gringo tourists?"

The men on the other boat spoke among themselves for a moment. Jacob waited, poised, wondering if they would be passed by.

Even if the pirates moved on, they still might spot the *Searunner* going to the real site of the wreck. It wasn't too far off. Would they be over the horizon from the false spot? Jacob wasn't sure.

Suddenly, the radio in the cabin let out a loud hiss.

"A jammer!" Jacob cried. "They're going to—"

The East African brought up an AK-47 and let out a burst over their heads. Everyone on the *Searunner* ducked.

"We're coming alongside you," the Berber said. "We want to search your ship and—"

He didn't get to finish his sentence. Néstor lifted up his rifle, braced it on the gunwale, and fired. The East African threw up his hands and fell back.

Jacob let out a burst from his MP5. A moment later, Jana rose up and got in on the action too.

The response seemed to take the pirates by surprise. They ducked down behind their own gunwale. Jacob saw the bullets spark off the side and knew that they had reinforced the steel to make it bulletproof, just like Néstor had done with the *Searunner*.

The pirates didn't stay cowed for long. Suddenly, a dozen of them popped up all along the side of the ship and opened fire. Most had Kalashnikovs, but some had more accurate rifles. Jacob and his companions ducked back down to avoid getting hit as a swarm of bullets panged off the gunwale and cabin.

Néstor had made the cabin bulletproof as well, and that proved to be a problem. Bullets ricocheted off the side of the cabin and some of them angled down to hit the deck, either punching through the wood or, if they hit a nail or support beam, angled up to bang into the back of the gunwale right next to them.

"Get inside the cabin!" Jacob shouted.

They rushed through the storm of lead, Néstor going to the pilot's cabin, Jacob and Jana rushing to the larger main cabin.

As they got inside, Jacob cast a glance at the tub, tucked beneath one of the bunks. It sat untouched, a steel lid Néstor had added firmly closed. Jacob didn't see any blood on the floor. Good. The kid had made it in time.

That wouldn't save her if the pirates boarded.

Damn, I've endangered another innocent. What's wrong with me?

He got to a porthole and found he didn't have to open it. The glass had already been shot out. He leveled his MP5 and gave a short, controlled burst at the opposing ship. Jana opened her porthole and started firing single shots with her M16. He could hear the regular crack of Néstor's rifle from the pilot's cabin.

Bullets continued to hammer against the *Searunner*. Their return fire wasn't having any effect. For a moment, it looked like a standoff. The more numerous pirate crew couldn't close and try to board without taking heavy losses, and the three of them couldn't drive them off.

Then Jacob made a lucky hit with his MP5, a pirate falling out of sight behind the gunwale. A few seconds later, a pirate to the right clapped a hand to his shoulder and ducked down, probably hit by Jana.

At a command Jacob couldn't hear through the gunfire, the pirates all ducked down behind the gunwale again.

"You think we scared them off?" Jana asked.

"Their engine is still idling," Néstor called from the cabin. "They're not going anywhere."

"They're planning something," Jacob said. "Everybody get ready."

There was a clattering of metal as everyone aboard the *Searunner* reloaded.

Just as Jacob snapped a fresh magazine into his submachine gun, his prediction came true.

With a shout, the pirate crew rose as one and fired a volley into the side of the ship. Jacob fired back, then noticed that a little to his right one of the pirates held a rocket-propelled grenade.

"Get the guy with the RPG!" Jacob shouted, shifting his aim, and letting off a long burst at him.

Too late. The RPG fired, there was a blur of motion between the ships, and an ear-splitting thud as the RPG hit. The entire ship shuddered, and the pirates let out a cheer.

The firing died down from the pirate ship. Several of the crew ducked back out of sight.

Néstor ran into the main cabin from the pilot's cabin.

"Crap!" he shouted. He spared a glance at the tub, saw it was all undamaged, and ran to the back of the cabin.

"Is it bad?" Jacob called over his shoulder, sending another burst at the pirate vessel.

The captain opened a hatch leading to the lower hold.

"Damn it!" Néstor shouted. "The bastards hit us below the waterline. We're taking on water."

CHAPTER FOURTEEN

Jacob cursed as Néstor ran back into the pilot's cabin. A few more bullets panged off the side of the ship.

The ship's pumps started a regular thumping below their feet.

"Is that going to be enough?" Jacob called.

Néstor didn't reply, because at that moment, the pirate captain called over.

"You're sinking. Surrender now and we'll spare your lives."

Jacob looked back at the tub where the captain's young daughter hid. Then he looked over at Jana.

"Not going to happen," the archaeologist said.

Néstor put his head back inside the main cabin. "Let them get close, and then we'll let them have it."

Jacob looked in his eyes. "I'm sorry."

Néstor gave him a grin. "We've been through worse and made it through."

He moved over to the tub, opened it a crack, and said, "Stay put, honey. We're in for some rough stuff."

"OK, Dad," Eva replied, sounding less worried than Jacob felt.

Jacob crouched down and rummaged through his duffel bag, pulling out two grenades with red rings painted on their tops.

"When they get close," he told his companions, "cover me and I'll give them a nasty surprise."

Néstor gave him a thumbs up, then moved back into the pilot's cabin.

"We surrender!" he called over to the pirates. "We'll lay down our arms if you promise not to kill us."

"All right. We don't want any more bloodshed. Drop your weapons over the side."

"Damn, now what do we do?" Jana said.

"Hold on," Néstor said, reappearing again and rummaging around in a footlocker. He pulled out three old rifles. "Got these off of the last guys who tried to steal my ship. Never thought I'd have much use for them."

He moved to the porthole and shouted. "Only one of us is coming out of cover. You'll see me throw all three guns overboard, then I'm getting back inside."

There was a short pause.

"Fair enough, but if you pull anything, we'll blow you out of the water."

Néstor gave Jacob an uncertain look and moved out on deck. He held the rifles high and one by one threw them into the water. He didn't waste a moment getting back into the bulletproof cabin.

"Let's hope that works," he said, moving back to his post in the pilot's cabin.

The overpowered engine of the trawler started up, and the ship turned toward them in order to move alongside.

"OK, I'm going out there," Jacob said once they drew a bit closer.

"Good luck," Jana said.

"Thanks." *I'll need it.*

He had the grenades stuffed in his back pockets.

Leaving his MP5 by the door, he moved out of the back of the cabin, hands held high.

Several men stood by the gunwale of the pirate ship. Their guns zeroed in on him the instant he appeared.

"Whoa! We don't want any trouble," Jacob shouted.

"For someone who doesn't want trouble, you sure are prepared for it," the pirate captain said. "Your cabin is bulletproof."

Um, yeah, that's kind of hard to explain.

"We're in the import/export business," Jacob said.

"What you got on board?"

"A shipment of cocaine."

"It's ours now," one of the crew said. The others laughed.

They were almost alongside now. Twenty meters. Ten.

Jacob pulled out one of the grenades, yanked the pin, and tossed it.

The pirates reacted faster than he expected. Three of them opened up before the grenade made it halfway to the ship. He had to duck back through the doorway, or he would have been cut down in another moment.

He heard a loud bang in the other ship, yanked the second grenade from his pocket, pulled the pin, and kept low as he ran out of the doorway. He moved a few yards toward the stern, keeping out of sight before popping up and chucking the second grenade.

By then, the first one was already causing chaos.

It was an incendiary grenade, and its explosion had set a good three-yard patch of the ship into a roaring blaze. Several of the pirates ran around screaming.

Jacob smiled as he ducked back down and crawled into the cabin again. Nothing panicked a group of sailors as much as a fire on board.

The second grenade went off. A terrible shriek told him he'd caught someone in its blast.

Néstor and Jana opened up with their guns.

Jacob grabbed his MP5 and peeked out his porthole. The pirates had gotten out of sight again, and Jacob could hear the whoosh of a fire extinguisher. One of the big patches of flames began to dwindle.

Jana rushed over and started looking inside his munitions bag.

"Why didn't you bring any more?"

"Sorry."

"Men never know how to pack." Jana looked around and noticed a flare gun hanging from a bracket on the wall. "Hey, this might keep them scared. Maybe even set fire to something."

She grabbed the flare gun, snapped a flare into place, and shot it out her porthole. It sailed over the stretch of water between the ships and landed out of sight.

"I think you might have overshot," Jacob said.

"No, that hit." Jana loaded the flare gun and fired a second time. "So did that."

The pirate vessel began to veer away. The three of them cheered.

Those cheers cut off abruptly as the guy with the RPG appeared again, only his head and shoulders visible, and fired again.

The rocket flew toward the ship, right for the waterline.

No way we can survive another hit.

A second explosion rocked the *Searunner*. As the roaring faded in his ears, Jacob heard a far worse sound—silence.

The pumps had shut off.

"The power's gone!" Néstor shouted. "I'll connect the emergency generator."

Jacob emptied his magazine at the retreating ship, not that he expected to hit anything, just firing out of pure spite. The first patch of flames was all but extinguished, and the second was diminishing. Obviously, the crew had gotten to work with several fire extinguishers, kneeling behind the gunwale to keep from making themselves targets. Thin columns of smoke came up from a couple of other places where

Jana had hit with her flare gun, but those would be put out soon enough.

They had lost the battle, and now the *Searunner* was listing noticeably to starboard.

Jacob rushed over to the hatch the captain had opened and looked down. He saw a cargo hold loaded with a few steel footlockers and rapidly filling with water. Without any lights down there, he couldn't see more. Couldn't see how bad the holes were.

Judging from the steady rise of the water level, they were bad enough.

"Néstor! You better get those pumps working!"

"There's a problem with the emergency power," the captain shouted back. "Hold on."

"They're picking up speed," Jana said, still looking out the porthole.

Jacob moved over beside her and looked out too. The armored fishing trawler's powerful engine was churning up water and moving away, heading for the location of the wreck.

The location on the map or the actual location of the wreck? The spots were too close together for Jacob to tell, and he had more immediate problems at the moment.

"What if they swing around and ram us?" Jana said.

"I don't think so. We're sinking, and they're in a hurry. That's good enough."

"But we're after the treasure too."

"They don't know that. As far as they're concerned, we were just in the wrong place at the wrong time. They didn't want any witnesses. After we turned out to be armed and armored, they probably believed that story about us being drug runners. They won't worry about us calling Mayday once that jammer is out of range, not with a ship full of cocaine."

"Anything we can do?" Jana shouted into the pilot's cabin.

"Check the lifeboat," Néstor called back. "It's strapped to the stern."

That wasn't the answer either of them wanted to hear.

A creaking sound made them turn. The lid of the tub opened up, and a ferret and a teenage girl peeked out.

"Are they gone?" Eva asked.

"Yes," Jana said. "Are you OK?"

"Yeah, but the ship isn't," Eva said, hopping out. Davey Jones hopped out, too, pattered around in the water that was just beginning to film the floor of the cabin, and scampered up to higher ground.

"Eva, is that you?" Néstor called. "Come in here and help with this connector."

"Coming!"

Jacob and Jana ran out to the stern. The boat was listing even more now. In a few more minutes, it would capsize or just sink completely.

An inflatable, four-man dingy was strapped to the stern in a protective steel case, a powerful motor set nearby. Both looked unharmed, although the gunwale right next to it was pockmarked from the impacts of bullets.

Just as Jacob was about to call back to the crew, the pumps came back online.

"Good job!" he shouted, rushing back inside.

"My dad's useless with electronic stuff," Eva said, coming back in from the pilot's cabin. She held a pair of buckets. "We're going to need to give those pumps a little help."

They formed a bucket line, with Jacob scooping up water from the open hatch, passing the bucket to Eva, who passed it to Jana at the doorway, who ran over to the side of the ship and tossed the water overboard.

"This doesn't solve our main problem," Jacob said.

"We need to get the waterline low enough for Dad to get down there."

They kept at it, working up a sweat, the waterline going down far too slowly. Once when Jana returned from outside, she reported the pirate ship had made it almost out of sight.

"Néstor," Jacob called as he filled another bucket, "call a Mayday signal."

"Hell, no," the captain said, coming into the main cabin with two large packages under his arm. "What do I tell the Coast Guard? Plus, the gunfire knocked out our radio, so I can't even if I wanted to. Anyway, I can fix this."

"What are those?" Jana asked.

"You'll see."

Néstor clambered down into the hold and moved out of sight, keeping his head in the narrow breathing space between the waterline and the roof.

After a moment, he ducked out of sight.

A surge of water shot out of the hatch.

"Damn! What happened?" Jacob said. The waterline was almost to the roof of the hold again.

Eva only laughed. "Dad's fixing the leak."

"Looks like he's making it worse."

Néstor appeared a moment later, soaked and sputtering. "One down. One to go."

He took a deep breath and went below again.

"They're tough, inflatable plugs," Eva explained. "A capsule of compressed gas inflates them, and the rubbery stuff they're made of fills the gap. That's why the water shoots up. It's displacing a bunch of it."

A second geyser of water shot out of the hatch, followed by their captain, coughing, and wiping his eyes.

Eva grabbed his hand and helped him out. "Good job, Dad."

"They're both plugged. Now we can let the pump do its work," Néstor said.

"Can we sail with those things plugging the gaps?" Jacob asked.

The teenager rolled her eyes. "Obviously not, dummy. The force of the water would push them out of the holes."

"Yeah, obviously," Jana parroted, rolling her eyes too.

"Oh, great. Sarcasm in stereo," Jacob muttered.

Jana frowned at him. "Instead of worrying about your fragile ego, how about you worry about the fact that we're dead in the water, and the pirates are heading for the wreck?"

"The wrong spot for the wreck."

"We don't know that for sure."

"Take the lifeboat and go after them," Eva said.

"What?" all three adults replied in unison.

"Honey, if we stay here the pirates might come back for us," her father said. "We need to use that lifeboat to get back to shore."

"They won't come back. They're after the treasure. And the safest thing for us would be for Jacob and Jana to go get the treasure first, and maybe sink the pirate ship with those plastic explosives he's got in his bag."

"You looked in my bag?" Jacob said.

"Duh. You're a walking disaster. I need to know what I'm up against."

"Since when am I a walking disaster?"

98

"Since the last time you came down here and we nearly got eaten by sharks."

Néstor laughed. "True enough, kiddo. But you forgot one thing. If they take the lifeboat, how do we get back to shore?"

"If we put up only quarter sail, we'll go slow enough that the force of the water might not dislodge the plugs."

"Risky."

"They'll probably leak a bit, but we have the pump. And I'll be back there with a bucket."

Néstor turned to Jacob. "See what I mean? Already as good of a sailor as I am."

"Better," Eva said. "Way better."

"Don't get ahead of yourself. Take the lifeboat, Jacob."

"You sure?"

The captain put his arm around his daughter. "I'm sure."

"Jana can stay here and help."

"Excuse me?"

"I've put you in enough risk as it is," Jacob said.

"This is just as much my mission as it is yours."

"Since when?"

"Since you disrupted my life yet again. Let's move out."

Jana   headed   for   the   stern   to   set   up   the   dingy.

CHAPTER FIFTEEN

Jana scanned the horizon and saw no sign of the pirates, or any other ship. Although the Caribbean was a busy sea, they were off the main shipping lanes.

What she did see were the two islands drawn on the chart. They were getting close. Thanks to the chart, and a GPS Jacob had brought along, they sped along in the dingy toward the true spot of the wreck of the *Santo Santiago*.

Now, Jana felt sure the pirates were on the wrong track. They hadn't seen the ship since they had left the *Searunner*.

The dingy, built to carry four, was crowded with scuba gear, weapons, and provisions for three days. Jana hoped the food and water would last. They had left most with Néstor and Eva just in case they couldn't use the sail without dislodging the plugs.

Good thing the hull had been armored, otherwise the ship would have been torn in half. They would have all been killed. Or captured.

She didn't even want to think about what they would have done to Eva.

Damn him, she thought, looking at Jacob as he sat in the stern, one hand on the tiller and the other on the GPS. *He doesn't care who he endangers, does he? If I had known there was a teenager on that vessel, I would have never agreed to set sail. I would have taken the map and left.*

She looked at the map and at the islands again. One was bigger and closer than the other, a rocky eminence with a covering of moss, grass, and a couple of scraggly trees. The second island was much smaller, barely more than a boulder sticking out of the sea.

Both showed clearly on the map, though. They were almost there.

A modern chart of the region that she had purchased in Caracas revealed what lay beneath the waves. Those two islands were peaks in an underwater ridge. A large, relatively flat area only forty meters below the surface stretched out from the larger island to encompass the area right below them.

She turned to Jacob. The questions that had been troubling her all this time now bubbled to the surface.

100

"Look, if we find the shipwreck, we're going to be so occupied with it that we won't have time to talk. So, before we start diving for it, I have a couple of questions."

"Don't worry. I know how to scuba dive."

"Of course you do. They teach you how to do everything in that damn organization. That's not what I'm asking. I mean I have questions about my father and about you."

"Your father was a good man."

"A good operative, sure. You kind of misled me about how well you knew him. You made it sound like he gave you a bit of training, but when I got his things, I found a bunch of photos of you together. Looks like you spent a lot of time with him."

Jacob's eyes got shifty. "A bit, yeah."

"More than I did," Jana grumbled.

"Oh, that's not true. He always looked forward to going back to the States and visiting you."

"Yeah, *visiting* me. Like I was some niece living in another country. I bet he didn't *visit* you. He hung out with you every day for years."

Jacob shook his head. "Not quite."

"And now you won't even tell me what you were up to!" The old jealousy was coming back, putting an adolescent whine into her voice.

Jana refused to feel embarrassed by that. Why shouldn't she complain? It was an old hurt, never healed, and this selfish, annoying man in the boat next to her refused to even talk about it.

"You know all that's classified," Jacob said, sounding impatient.

"The barbeques are classified?" Jana snapped. "The fishing trips are classified?"

"Rest breaks during training missions."

"No, they weren't, or Dad wouldn't have taken photos."

"Look, he cared about you, all right? He—"

"He skipped my birthdays! I have a photo of him celebrating one of yours."

"Oh. That. Yeah, um, we were on a mission."

"Mission, mission, mission. I'm so sick of you people talking about your damn missions!"

"You have to understand that some stuff is classified."

Jana felt the rage rising in her. "What about your name? Is that classified?"

Jacob jerked a little. "Huh?"

101

"At the Dome of the Rock, remember? Some American guy recognized you and called you Mitch. He looked military. You pretended you didn't hear."

"I didn't hear that," Jacob mumbled. "He must have mistook me for someone else."

"Ugh!" Jana shoved him. Jacob, surprised at the move, toppled off the side of the boat with a splash.

"Serves you right, asshole!"

Jana grabbed the tiller and circled the dingy around. When he came up, perhaps she'd circle around some, make him swim for a while. That might jog his memory.

He lies and lies. He pulls her along into missions she's not prepared for, missions that take her away from her life and could even end it, and he doesn't have the decency to speak the truth, not even about her father!

Yeah, let him swim for a while.

He hadn't come up. She circled around again, looking for him. The spot where he had gone down was placid. No bubbles came to the surface.

She cut the engine.

"Jacob?" she called, even though she knew he couldn't hear.

She looked all around. No sign of him.

"Jacob!"

Nothing.

Oh no. Did he get a cramp or something?

Jacob's head and shoulders popped out of the water a few yards away from the dingy. He shook his head and spat out some seawater, reminding her of the statue of Poseidon she had seen outside Madrid.

"Stop fooling around, you idiot!" Jana said. "You—"

She almost said that he had scared her but cut off at the last moment. She wouldn't give him the satisfaction.

"I found it!" Jacob shouted.

"What?"

"The ship! I found it. It's right below us."

"Really?"

The old map, while showing a precise location, was of a scale that made the spot encompass a good quarter square mile.

"You sure?"

"Yeah!" Jacob said, swimming for the boat. Jana got ready to motor away again.

"You're not just saying that to get back in the boat?"

"No. You got grumpy just at the right time. I knew it was a good idea to bring you along."

"Ugh!" Jana started up the motor and sped away.

"Hey!"

"Stay where you are to mark the spot. Act like a buoy. It should be easy because you always act like a boy."

"That's a dad joke!" Jacob shouted. "Only Néstor is allowed to say dad jokes!"

Jana ran a wide circle around him, then decided to do a second lap. More slowly this time. Jacob stayed where he was, treading water.

At last, she came back to him.

"Truce?" Jacob said, flashing what he thought was a winning smile.

Jana killed the engine. "We got to get this thing before the pirates realize they're in the wrong spot and start searching the area. Get in."

Jacob clambered aboard, stripped off his soaked clothing down to his underwear, and started to pull on a wetsuit. Jana reached for hers too.

"You need to stay up here in case there's trouble," Jacob said.

"Yeah, I guess you're right." As much as she wanted to go down there, she hadn't been scuba diving for years, and if they both went down there, the dingy might drift too far away.

Plus, she really didn't want to strip to her underwear in front of Jacob.

"Ever excavate a sunken ship?" Jacob asked.

"Underwater archaeology is an entirely different discipline," Jana replied, forgetting her anger with him in the anticipation of their discovery. "I only learned scuba diving to visit some wrecks. I never actually worked on one."

"Any advice?"

"You're looking for a small chest. It will be padded on the inside and contain a glass sphere."

Jacob looked at her. "A glass sphere?"

"In the archives in Caracas, I discovered a letter by one of Sebastián de Ulloa's colleagues, saying the physician had extracted samples of air from the lungs of several patients dying of Black Fever. He compressed them using one of the first-ever air compressors and injected the air into a glass sphere that he sealed. If the sphere hasn't broken, the virus should still be inside."

"That's a big if. Why didn't you tell me all this before?"

"So much was going on, I didn't have time."

Jacob studied her a moment. Jana felt herself flush. He got back to work hooking up his gear.

There had been plenty of time—during the drive to the coast, or walking to the secret pier, or when they were sailing on the *Searunner*. The truth was, Jana didn't want to tell him. He kept so many secrets from her, she wanted to keep a secret from him, at least until he needed to know it.

After a moment, Jacob asked, "Would it still be viable?"

Jana shrugged, looking out over the water. "I'm not sure. I've heard viruses and bacteria can go dormant for a very long time and survive very adverse conditions. There were even experiments on the International Space Station leaving samples out in the cold vacuum of space, and they survived."

"Damn. I was kind of hoping the pirates were following a pipe dream."

"God, I hope so. We can't bet on that, though. Get down there and find it before the pirates discover they're following the wrong map."

Jacob grabbed one of the air tanks. "Will do. Damn it!"

"What?"

"This one's empty. Look, it got dinged by a bullet. That must have created a leak."

Jana clenched her teeth. "What about the other one?"

He checked the gauge. "This one got dinged too. It must be a slow leak, though, because it's still got forty minutes of air left."

"Will it be OK under the pressure of deep water?"

"I sure hope so. Probably, since the water pressure will be pushing in and not out. It might seal the thing. Or water might start leaking into the tank. I'll know soon enough. Anyway, I better find that chest of yours pretty damn quick."

He strapped on the tank, put on his face mask and mouthpiece, and gave her a wave before diving backwards off the boat.

Within a moment, he had sunk out of sight.

Jana sat there, feeling helpless. For all his training, Jacob had no experience looking around old shipwrecks. He hadn't even mentioned ever visiting one. At least she had done that, and her archaeological training would help too. She should have gone down. Not him.

She checked her watch. He'd only been down there for a couple of minutes. No, almost four minutes. A tenth of his air gone. How could he ever find Ulloa's chest in less than an hour?

Those worries vanished, replaced by a new one as she saw the prow of a ship come out from beyond the larger of the two islands nearby.

She stared, frozen, as she recognized the fishing trawler with its armored hull pockmarked by the impact of bullets.

It was the pirate ship. They must have gone to the spot on the map, realized it was wrong, and sailed on a search pattern until they spotted the dingy.

And now, she had to face them alone. She grabbed her M16.

No, that would be suicide. She needed to run. Jacob was safe for the moment underwater. Maybe if she could lead them on a chase, get them away from this spot, she could circle around and pick him up.

She put the engine at full throttle and sped across the water, heading for the shore that she knew lay just out of sight beyond the southern horizon. Maybe if she got in sight of some other ships, the pirates wouldn't fire on her.

Jana hunched low to make herself less of a target, the warm Caribbean wind hitting her face. She looked over her shoulder and cursed. The pirates had passed the spot of the wreck and were chasing her just like she wanted, but that powerful engine was churning up the water, rapidly reducing the distance between them. Several men stood at the prow, weapons ready.

She kept going, hoping to buy Jacob some time.

She didn't buy him much of it. Bullets kicked up the water to her right, then again to her left.

Warning shots.

She looked over her shoulder again. The converted fishing trawler was almost upon her. The men had stopped firing warning shots.

Now, they were aiming at her.

She cut the engine. There was no point in running.

They had caught her.

CHAPTER SIXTEEN

Jacob had gone scuba diving all over the world—the Mediterranean, the Caribbean, the Great Barrier Reef—and the underwater world had never ceased to amaze him. You plunged below the surface, and all fell silent but for the sound of your own breathing. All the world you knew vanished, all its fights and tensions, and got replaced with a clear, quiet place full of strange creatures.

The tropics was the best place to dive, and the waters off the coast of Venezuela didn't disappoint. He descended through schools of colorful fish like living paintings. One was made up of hundreds of tiny fish like slivers of silver all moving in unison, catching the light. Another, smaller school was made up of fish of a canary yellow, with brilliant blue and red strips along their length. Some larger fish swam alone, sedately showing off colors that could rival that of any tropical bird.

Suffused with wonder, Jacob forgot the argument back on the boat, and the dangers they had just been through. Even his own buoyancy eased his many bruises and sprained wrist, making him forget the bomb blast back in Greece. For the next forty minutes, he would be at peace.

He should really scuba dive more often. It always made him feel better. The world was a relentless enemy, and for a time, he could forget that down here.

A magical place, and nothing was more magical than the pure luck that had brought him to this spot. When Jana had pushed him off the boat, he had dived as deep as he could just to scare her. What he never expected was that he would see the outline of the old ship as clear as day on the bottom.

Now, equipped with an oxygen tank and swimming deeper than before, he could see it much more clearly. The ship lay half-covered with silt, its twin masts fallen and crisscrossed across its hull.

Even at this distance, he could see it was an eighteenth-century fighting ship. It looked like a frigate or one of the smaller ships of the line, built not for one of the great navies of the time but for fighting civilian vessels. He could see the portholes for cannons on the deck and supposed more lay beneath the surface.

The map hadn't lied. This was no civilian transport. This was definitely the *Santo Santiago* and not the *Nueva Esperanza*.

He continued to descend, pacing himself so his body got used to the change in pressure. He didn't even bother to look back up at the surface. That world could wait for a while. A boyhood dream lay just below him.

The *Santo Santiago* grew clearer as he ventured farther beneath the waves. He could see damage now. One porthole had been smashed, and the wrecked husk of the cannon still lay at its post, shattered by a well-aimed cannonball. He didn't see the other cannons, though. Had they been looted? Had divers discovered this wreck, kept it a secret, and plundered it?

He tried to keep that unpleasant possibility out of his mind. As Aaron Peters always used to say, *"Focus on the problem in front of you and don't invent new ones in your head."*

The problem in front of him was that he needed to explore a large, 250-year-old shipwreck looking for a small chest. Didn't Jacques Cousteau and all those people spend years clearing out wrecks like this?

Jacob got right above the wreck and swam in place for a time, studying it. It was in remarkable shape, the main damage coming not from the ravages of time but from whatever battle had sunk it. He could see more damage from cannonballs now. The side was peppered with holes, and a big one right in the center of the deck. Fish swam in and out of its murky interior. He swam to its stern and saw raised lettering carved across the wood there. A few glinting spots hinted that it had once been adorned with gold paint. The letters were blurred with age, many obscured by barnacles, but he could make out that there were two words, the first starting with an S, and the second word having the letters "nti" in the center.

His heart beat faster. The *Santo Santiago*.

Jacob made a slow passage along the entire length of the deck, studying the battle damage under the light of his powerful headlamp. While the *Nueva Esperanza* might have fought back, there was no way a civilian ship could have battered a fighting vessel like this so badly. This was the work of another fighting ship.

The *Vengeance*? That had been the collector's theory.

But where the hell were all the cannons? Other than that smashed one, he didn't see any.

He didn't see much of anything on deck—no tools, no other equipment, or weapons. Just a length of heavy chain of the kind used to hold an anchor, one link of which had been twisted and snapped, perhaps from a cannonball. Perhaps the current had swept any smaller objects away, but it wouldn't have budged the cannons.

When he got to the prow, where a wooden mermaid encrusted with barnacles stared out over the bottom of the sea, he turned and headed back to the gaping hole in the deck.

He hesitated, savoring the moment, then plunged down into the unknown.

Jacob's eyes widened as he went below decks on a ship no one had sailed for more than two centuries.

The wonder he had felt swimming above the deck was nothing compared to the sensations he experienced as he swam inside the hull.

The silt had only filled it up about halfway. Jacob could see drifts that had moved in through the open portholes and battle damage, but which had then blocked those holes, keeping more particulates from entering. That left a wavy surface of sand filling up part of the space. A few crustaceans scuttled here and there.

Above was empty space between the sand and the upper deck. A large, blue fish glided by, staring at Jacob with an unblinking eye. Jacob swept his headlamp around to take in the ceiling encrusted with growths, a wooden staircase at the stern heading up to the top deck, and nothing else.

There were no cannons here either. No other objects that he could see. No skeletons.

They surrendered. The pirates surrendered to whomever beat them in battle. Then the victors plundered the ship and took off with the crew.

And did what with them? Kept them prisoner? Sold them as slaves? Threw them overboard?

There could be no answer to that. He picked a spot the farthest away from any battle damage—one where whatever had been on this deck wouldn't have been destroyed—and started digging in the sand with his hands.

The sand was loose, and with his legs braced against the ceiling, he could work quickly. But disturbing the sand created a giant cloud of it. Soon the entire lower deck filled with floating particles, obscuring his vision. He had to work by feel.

And his probing fingers, his sweeping hands, found nothing. He got all the way to the solid wood of the lower deck and cleared more space around it, still finding nothing.

Not so much as a sword or a marlinspike.

Whatever was on this ship is gone. Totally gone.

He checked his air gauge, bringing his face up close to see through the cloud he had created. Ten minutes. Time to go up. Jana would be disappointed, but it was mission accomplished. Either Sebastián de Ulloa's innovative isolation chamber for a deadly virus got broken in the battle, in which case both crews probably perished, or it was broken later with the same result. Or perhaps Ulloa explained what it was to his captors, and the cautious crew chucked it overboard.

Whatever happened, the sphere was gone. The pirates would find nothing. What he needed to do now was to get to the surface and get back to shore. If he alerted the Venezuelan coast guard about the presence of a pirate ship operating in the vicinity, maybe they could stop them. He'd alert the CIA too. They could track the ship via satellite.

Jana would insist on coming back to make a thorough check of the wreck. Fine by him. It would be fascinating. She had complained that he was taking her away from her career. Well, this would help her career. Maybe that would stop her whining and pushing him out of boats.

Maybe that would stop her from asking about her dad.

Yeah, right.

As he probed along the barnacled ceiling, looking for the hole back to the upper deck, he felt a deepening regret. He had rushed into this mission out of guilt for Gabriella's murder, hoping that saving the world would compensate for the death of his friend.

But he hadn't saved the world. All he'd done was kill a few lowlife pirates and endanger Néstor and his kid.

A bright spot in the gloom led him to the hole in the deck. He swam through it.

As he emerged from the cloud of silt he had created, two scuba divers swept in from either side of the hole. Strong hands grasped both his arms. The guy on his right arm clenched his injured wrist, sending a jab of pain all the way up to his shoulder. A third diver swam down from above. They had obviously been waiting for him.

One patted him down, removed the knife at his belt, and shook his head to the other two. Then he signaled to someone behind Jacob.

A fourth diver approached. He pulled out a writing slate and wrote, "Anything on him?"

The man who had searched him shook his head. The newcomer wrote, "Tie him up."

The pirates, Jacob said, vainly struggling. *They must have killed or captured Jana.*

The divers pulled him over to one of the fallen masts, a massive length of thick oak carved from a single tree. They took a length of old chain from the deck and wrapped it around the mast and then his legs, securing each leg to one of the links with a zip tie.

With a cheerful wave, they left him. Two began to search the deck while the other two plunged into the hole and went below.

Jacob pulled at his legs. No way was he going to get out of that. He looked up and saw a large shadow overhead and a bit to his left. *The pirate ship.* Damn, they led them right to the spot.

But there was nothing here. What would they do to him and Jana when they discovered that?

Torture them to answer questions they couldn't answer.

He checked his air gauge. It was already down to the red, reading eight minutes. There were usually a couple of minutes extra in them, but not much more than that. He looked around for something to use to cut the zip ties and saw nothing. It would be possible to unwind the chain from around the mast, but with his legs tied to the chain, he'd still be stuck. No way would he be able to swim to the surface with this massive length of iron.

The links were corroded and encrusted with barnacles. Maybe they would break if he hit them hard enough?

He picked up a length of the chain and smashed it as hard as he could against the mast. Water resistance reduced his force, and all he got was some scraped fingers and a throb of pain in his injured wrist. Giving this up, he began to unwind the chain. That would at least give him greater range of movement.

He kept an eye on the divers, who paid him little attention. The two swimming above the upper deck kept sweeping back and forth with their headlamps, finding nothing, just like he had found nothing.

Jacob's search, like theirs, resulted in frustration. There was no sharp bit of metal, no crowbar or anything similar, nothing he could use to cut those zip ties. His air was beginning to get stale. Each breath felt thin. Jacob resisted the urge to breathe deeper. He needed to conserve what little he had left.

The two divers who had gone below emerged from the deep. The two who had remained up above moved over to them, and they consulted for a moment, writing on their slates.

Then they came over to Jacob.

The one who appeared to be their leader wrote on his slate, "Do you know where the cave is?"

Huh?

Jacob gestured for him to hand over the writing slate. Once it was in his hands he wrote, "Bring me to the surface and I'll tell you."

He handed back the slate and the pirate wrote, "Tell us now."

He handed the slate back to him. "Bring me up first."

The pirate made a show of looking at his air gauge. At the very bottom of red. Then he wrote, "Want to breathe? Tell us where the cave is."

They stared at each other a moment. Jacob's mind raced as his lungs began to burn.

The pirate handed him back the slate. He fumbled the stylus. If it hadn't been attached to the slate by a cord it would have sunk to the deck.

"On the second iland, the one furter away. Hidden. I cn show u."

He looked at his own writing and could barely read it. He noticed a couple of spelling mistakes.

Loss of motor control. Foggy mind. I'm suffocating.

The diver looked at it, showed it to his companions, then wrote, "Wrong answer. You don't know shit. Enjoy your stay."

They began to ascend. Jacob reached for one, grasped a flipper, and felt it slide through his fingers as they rose up and away, disappearing back to the bright, airy world above that he knew he would never see again.

CHAPTER SEVENTEEN

Mounir Zerhouni studied the woman in front of him, the woman who had helped cause him so much trouble. She didn't look like much—scared, tired, her back against the railing and hemmed in by his crew. Helpless.

But not so helpless.

Yasir, his Somali, was dead. Two other good men were dead, too, and three more injured. One, Rigoberto, his Guatemalan navigator, lay writhing in pain on his bunk, covered in burns and begging to be released from his misery.

What terrible luck, to come so far and then run into some drug runners who punched way above their weight.

He had thought the ship was a simple pleasure craft that had strayed too close to the spot of the wreck and needed to be wiped out—a simple job that would take fifteen minutes. Instead, he had ended up in a battle.

This woman would pay. Pay dearly.

Braheem, a fellow Berber and his second-in-command, came up to him with an armful of documents he had taken from the dingy.

"They're not drug runners," he said in their native Amazigh so the prisoner wouldn't understand. "Look at this."

He held out a detailed nautical chart of the area and an old map identical to his own.

No, not identical. This map had a second set of coordinates that had been written in invisible ink, coordinates that led right here.

Mounir snorted. So, all his research had led him down the wrong path. He would have never found the wreck if he hadn't happened upon these people.

And who were these people? Obviously not what they said they were.

"What else was on the boat?" he asked Braheem.

"A GPS, an MP5, an M16, both with lots of ammo, a couple of 9mm pistols, and some C4."

No. Definitely not drug smugglers. You don't need plastic explosives to move cocaine.

Mounir studied the woman in front of him for a moment. He held up the old map. "Where did you get this?"

"I stole it."

"From whom?"

"A collector in Spain."

Mounir was about to ask who, then decided it didn't matter. He also decided not to ask her for her name or if they worked for a larger organization. Braheem also held their passports and wallets. As for who they might work for, she'd only lie about that. He could find out the truth later.

The crew would get it out of her. They already looked like they wanted to.

"Captain!" one of the crew called. "The divers have come up."

Mounir saw four heads bobbing in the water. Someone threw down a rope ladder, and one by one they climbed on board.

"Nothing, captain. The *Santo Santiago* is completely stripped. It's like you suspected."

Mounir nodded. In his long years of research, one of his great discoveries was a journal purporting to be that of the lone surviving crewman of the *Vengeance*, a pirate ship. The tale had inspired him so much he had named his own ship after that one. The journal told a fanciful tale of two rival pirate captains. The captain of the *Vengeance* had been horribly scarred in a duel with the captain of the *Santo Santiago* and had sworn revenge.

He had tracked the *Santo Santiago* to the Caribbean and found the ship, weighed heavily with treasure, and battered from a recent battle, sailing close to the shore of Venezuela. The captain of the *Vengeance* ordered his crew to open fire. There had been a bloody but quick battle. The gunners of the *Vengeance* proved to be superior, and soon the *Santo Santiago* was incapable of resistance, both her masts blown down and half her crew dead or injured.

The captain of the *Vengeance* gave them an offer—give up their captain to him as a prisoner, and they could join with his crew to replace his losses. The crew of the *Santo Santiago*, being pirates and having no loyalty to anyone but themselves, saw this as a good deal. Their captain was bound and gagged, sent over to the *Vengeance*, and made to walk the plank.

The captain of the *Vengeance*, delighted at this turn of events, kept his word, and welcomed the new crewmembers. It was the 1780s, the golden age of piracy had passed, and such men were at a premium.

113

Their first task was to transfer over all the booty of the *Santo Santiago* as well as all the guns, supplies, and tools. In the era before mass production, even a simple hammer had some real financial value.

The *Santo Santiago* was scuttled, and the *Vengeance* sailed on its way.

Not for long.

Soon the men from the *Santo Santiago* began to feel ill. Then they began to cough, and they developed a high fever. Shortly thereafter, they began to spit black phlegm.

It was the dreaded Black Fever. They must have caught it from someone on the *Nueva Esperanza*. The crew of the *Vengeance* threw all their new shipmates overboard, but it was too late. Soon the crew of the *Vengeance* had developed the symptoms too.

They sailed into a sea cave on an isolated stretch of coast they used as a hideout and hoped to wait out the disease. One by one, they all dropped dead.

Except for the man who wrote the journal. Miraculously, he had survived. He put this down to an intercession from God and promised to mend his evil ways. More likely, Mounir believed, he was fortunate enough to have natural immunity.

After the last of his shipmates had died, he left the cave, never to return. In his journal, he admitted to taking all the gold and jewels he could carry "in order to perform Godly works."

Yeah, right.

Mounir hadn't been sure what to make of this remarkable tale. It had never been printed, and the author remained anonymous, not even signing his own journal. Mounir had found no other evidence to corroborate the story. He had assumed it was fantasy, or at least highly exaggerated.

But now his divers told him the *Santo Santiago* had been stripped. Suddenly, the journal seemed a lot more believable.

The problem was, he hadn't found the cave. Mounir had been studying period charts and modern maps for more than a year just in case the journal turned out to be true, and he had narrowed it down to a certain stretch of coast, but he still hadn't found its precise location.

He turned again to look at the woman.

"What do you know about how the *Santo Santiago* sank?" he asked.

She shrugged. "Nothing. There are rumors that it was sunk by another pirate vessel called the *Vengeance*, but no one knows for sure. There's no evidence for it."

"Don't lie to me!" he snapped. "You know all about the cave."

The woman stared at him. He had said this deliberately to get a reaction. There was no flicker of recognition or deception in her eyes when she said, "I don't know what you're talking about."

Mounir studied her for a moment. She didn't get shifty or make a wide-eyed repetition of what she had previously said. She just stood there.

"Perhaps you're telling the truth," he said after a minute. "Unfortunately for you, I have to be certain."

He turned to two crewmen standing nearby. "You and you, take her below and make sure she talks."

The two men grinned and stepped toward the prisoner.

"No!"

The woman lashed out, kicking one man in the balls. As the pirate doubled over, letting out a falsetto shriek, the other dove for her. She gave him a right cross that would earn a nod of approval in any portside tavern, and with her other hand, she pulled out the knife in the sheath at his belt.

Cursing, Mounir took a step back and drew his .45 automatic. A bullet through the kneecap would change her attitude.

The prisoner slashed at his crewmember, who stumbled and got into Mounir's shot.

By the time Mounir had stepped to the right to get a clear line of fire, the woman had leapt onto the gunwale and dove into the sea.

Mounir rushed to the side of the ship. No trace of her.

"Hell with it," he said. "We have to find that cave. Sooner or later, someone's going to call the Coast Guard. Braheem, start the engines and head for the coast. Giorgos, Ridha, shoot the dingy. Those two can drown together."

Braheem ran to the helm, while the two seamen leaned over the gunwale and opened up with their automatics, peppering the rubber dingy full of holes.

It deflated in seconds. The weight of the engine dragged it under the surface.

As the *Vengeance* pulled away, heading south-southwest for the Venezuelan shore, Mounir stared at the spot around where it had gone down.

He didn't see either of the two Americans.

***

Jana's lungs burned as she swam with powerful strokes down toward the wreck of the *Santo Santiago*, her stolen dagger clenched in her teeth. She tried to ignore the coppery tang of the pirate's blood on the blade. Schools of colorful fish darted past. Far below, she could make out the vague shadow of the shipwreck.

She hadn't even gotten halfway down. Her dive from the deck had gotten her part of the way, but she hadn't managed to take in a good lungful of air before she entered the water, and that was costing her.

Jana tried to ignore the ache in her lungs and kept going.

There, about two-thirds of the way to the stern, was a dark shape against the lighter silt and a glint of something metallic. Jacob?

The pressure built up in her ears, feeling like the entire sea would burst through her eardrums to flood her skull. Her limbs began to tire. Black dots spotted her vision.

She couldn't make it. Impossible. She turned back, swimming upwards, helped by her own buoyancy, desperate to get back to the air. The space above her grew lighter. Almost there. God, how her lungs burned. Inhale. Just inhale.

Instinct kept her from doing it. She transferred the knife from her mouth to her hand in anticipation of that first breath, and almost slipped and inhaled too soon. She had to bite on her lips to keep them from betraying her.

The water above her grew brighter and brighter until, at last, she burst to the surface to cough out the stale contents of her lungs and take a deep gulp of life.

Only to inhale some seawater too.

Choking, coughing, flailing her arms, she struggled to breathe and stay afloat.

Come on, get it together. Jacob is running out of air.

Finally, she cleared her lungs and began taking deep breaths in preparation for another dive. She ducked her head under the surface, adjusted her position until she was treading water right over the stern of the wreck, and took some more deep breaths.

Then she descended as fast as she could.

The wreck grew more visible beneath her. Her head began to feel the pressure and her lungs began to demand air. She kept going.

The charts said it was forty meters down. Could she really dive forty meters without oxygen?

116

By the time she got halfway down, she realized the answer was no. Jacob looked up at her, reaching up for help she knew she couldn't give. He floated not far from one of the masts, apparently tied to a heavy chain.

Keep swimming. Keep swimming.

She couldn't. Her lungs demanded air. Her muscles were weakening. She stopped, waved the knife, hoping he would see it, and dropped it to him. It pirouetted in the water as it fell.

Praying he'd get it and it would be what he needed, she turned and swam for the surface, laden with the guilt that she might have failed.

CHAPTER EIGHTEEN

Jana treaded water, taking deep breaths. Shouldn't he have come up by now?

She dove back down, struggling to get down to the wreck, but her body gave up at less of a depth than her previous two attempts.

Jacob was still at the wreck. She returned to the surface.

Her muscles were beginning to tire. She got into a dead man's float and tried to rest. At least the sea was fairly calm. A current moved her away from the wreck, and after a minute, she had to swim a little to get back over it.

If he doesn't come up soon, I'll have to leave him. I might not reach that island even now.

She risked one more dive. As she did, she saw him swimming up. Jana swam down to meet him. Again, her muscles and lungs protested, but she ignored them. Jacob's movements appeared weak, uncoordinated. He was floating more than swimming.

But he rose just enough for her to grab him. Pulling off his tank and discarding it to give him more buoyancy, she lifted him back to the surface, making it just in time to take in air in a series of grateful gasps.

"You OK, Jacob?" she managed to say.

Jacob didn't respond.

"Jacob?" She shook him. "Hey, Jacob!"

He lay in her arms, unmoving, eyes a pair of unfocused slits.

"Damn it!" She got behind him, wrapped her arms around his middle, and squeezed.

A jet of water came out of his mouth, along with some bile and vomit.

She slapped him on the cheek, splashed some water in his face. Still nothing.

She was certified in first aid and CPR, but she had never given mouth to mouth resuscitation for real, and certainly never while treading water way too far from land.

Pinching his nose, she locked her lips with his and breathed into his mouth. She pulled away, struggling to keep him in position while treading water, and breathed into his mouth a second time.

She kept at it even as she felt her muscles weaken.

Suddenly, after a couple of minutes of this treatment, he coughed, sputtered in her face, and took a breath on his own.

Jana kept holding him, treading water, waiting until he could do so for himself.

"You OK?"

He nodded.

"I'm going to take your flippers and help you swim to the islands, all right?"

He nodded again.

Jana switched the flippers from her feet to his. As she did this, Jacob managed to tread water on his own. A good sign, but she could tell he'd never make it to the island under his own power.

She wasn't sure she could, either.

"You sure you're OK?" she asked again.

"Besides a raging headache (gasp!) and complete exhaustion (gasp!) I'm fine."

"Let's go."

Jana did a backstroke with Jacob holding onto her middle and pushing weakly with his own legs. Their limbs kept getting tangled, but they made some progress.

Too little. After a few minutes, she looked over her shoulder, and the island looked almost as distant as before. Even worse, the current was pulling them at an angle away from it. They might miss landfall entirely.

No choice but to go on. They kept swimming, angling to the right to counteract the current.

So began a nightmare of fatigue, a bleary endurance contest against the currents and waves. Jacob rallied a little, helping her more, but he never got the strength to let go. It was up to Jana to get them through.

"If your team is relying on you, there is no greater responsibility," her father always used to say. *"Sacrifice everything, go to any lengths, for the people who would do the same for you."*

She kept swimming, swimming until her mind was an agonized blank and the pain in her muscles became so great that they took over her entire being.

They were both so out of it that they didn't even see the shore until they banged against the rocks.

They let go of each other and tried to grasp at the slippery stone. The waves banged them up against them a second time, then pulled

119

them away before their numb hands could grab a hold. Jana saw a cleft between two stones a little to their right, one that narrowed before ending at the rocky, rising slope of the island.

She made for it. Jacob followed. The next wave washed them right into it. Jana moved her body so that it jammed into the cleft, her knee smacking against a submerged stone, and her forehead cracking against the side.

Yet she managed to hold on. She braced herself, resting for a moment.

When she looked around, she didn't see Jacob.

"Jacob?" she called, so weakly she could barely hear herself.

A wave pushed her against the rocks. With the last of her strength, she struggled up out of the water, flopped down, then just managed to raise her head to blearily look around.

Jacob lay on a smooth stone not far off, face down, the water lapping at his feet.

After a minute, they summoned the strength to crawl to each other, touching hands before slipping into unconsciousness on the dry land.

***

Jana didn't know how long she lay on the edge of the island, but when she awoke, her skin burned, and her throat was a raging desert of thirst. The sun had moved in the sky, and Jacob lay on his side, eyes open, looking at her.

"You OK?" he croaked.

"No. And you?"

"Alive. Thanks."

"You're lucky you didn't get the bends."

"That only becomes a risk after thirty minutes. I wasn't down much more than that."

Jana struggled to stand but could barely sit.

"We're getting sunburned. That will make us more dehydrated."

"There are a couple of trees up that hill. Let's get to them."

They began to crawl. They made it only a quarter of the way before their bodies gave out.

Lying on her front, gasping into the rocky soil, Jana knew she was at the very end of her strength. Jacob couldn't be any better. He had nearly drowned.

"What do we do?" Jana moaned.

"Rest a bit and try again."

That hadn't really been her question. What she meant to ask was, how the hell did they get off this island? It was out of sight of the mainland, and they didn't even have the energy to stand up, let alone fashion some sort of raft from the trees, and make an attempt at sailing back to Venezuela. Not that they had the tools to do that.

They were marooned.

After a few minutes, they began to crawl up the slope again, trying to reach the shade to spare their already red skin.

Jana knew that would only prolong their suffering. This island was too small to have any water, and it wouldn't be long before dehydration knocked them out.

After that, it would only be a matter of time.

The cry of seagulls behind them sounded like a death knell. Would they pick on their bodies once she and Jacob died? Would some fisherman find them days from now, bodies bloated, the soft parts eaten away by birds?

The cries grew louder, more insistent.

Damn, they're closing in already. Maybe it isn't seagulls. Maybe there's some sort of buzzard in these parts that goes after dying animals.

Her hand fumbled around for a loose stone she could use to fend them off, knowing in her heart that if a flock of scavengers swopped down on her, there was nothing she could do to keep from dying a horrible death.

CHAPTER NINETEEN

Jana rolled onto her back, holding up the stone, ready to smack any buzzard that ventured close.

But she saw no birds.

The call continued. Her mind, activated by the instinct to fight, cleared enough that she recognized a human voice.

She struggled to prop herself up on her elbows ...

... and couldn't believe what she saw.

The *Searunner*, under a quarter sail, moved slowly a few hundred yards off the island's shore. Eva stood on the prow, her long, black hair streaming in the breeze, waving, and calling their names.

"Jacob," Jana said.

"Ugh. Another minute," he mumbled, his face on the ground.

"Jacob, look!"

He looked at her, then followed her gaze.

"You seeing that?" Jana asked.

"Yeah," he said, perking up. "Wow, yeah I do."

"So, it's not a hallucination?"

"If it is, we're both having it."

Jana waved, only just managing not to fall over, as the *Searunner* turned toward the island and sailed for them.

***

Jana and Jacob lay in opposite bunks in the *Searunner's* cabin. Néstor was at the helm, sailing for the mainland, while Eva tended to them. She had tucked them in, put some cream on their burned skin, and given them plenty of water. Now, she was brewing up some tea and ramen in the ship's small kitchenette. Davey Jones lay curled on Jana's chest, studying her with his little black eyes, his whiskers twitching.

"How's the ship?" Jana managed to croak out.

The pumps made a rhythmic thudding beneath the deck.

"The plugs are holding, more or less," the girl said as she fussed around the kitchen. "I'll have to get to work with the bucket pretty soon."

"Sorry for all this trouble," Jacob said.

Eva laughed. "Since when do you say sorry for causing trouble?"

Jacob's face turned grim. "I've caused too much of it lately."

Jana knew he was talking about his friend who had been killed. The girl didn't, however, and continued brightly, "That's OK, Jacob. You make life interesting."

"Too interesting," he mumbled.

"Aw, you're just depressed because you got your ass kicked. Dad says you got to take the losses with the wins."

Sounds like something my dad would say, Jana thought.

"My dad said the same thing," Jacob replied. Jana glanced at him.

The girl brought over two steaming mugs of tea. Jana and Jacob struggled to sit.

"I put extra sugar in them. And whole milk too. You guys need it. The ramen is coming up in a minute. Sorry I can't cook anything better. Everyone says my mom was a great cook, but I don't remember her. So, who's going to teach me? My dad? Ha! He can barely boil water."

Jacob took the tea mug, then reached out and held the girl's hand.

"Your mother would be proud of you."

"You think?" the girl asked, sounding touched.

"I know."

"You didn't know her. You told me once."

"I didn't need to know her. The kind of woman who would marry your father would definitely be proud of how you turned out."

"Crazy, you mean," Eva said with a bright laugh. She squeezed Jacob's hand, then turned and gave Jana her tea. "How are you doing?"

"I feel like your ship," Jana replied.

"Drink your tea. Food's up in a minute." She bent to scratch Davey Jones behind the ears. "You take care of them, OK?"

She walked back to the kitchenette.

Jana studied Jacob for a moment. That little interaction with Eva had shown another side of him. Only once before had she seen him being tender with a kid before, giving a young person reassurance and support. She hadn't thought him capable.

He sipped his tea, looking at nothing, lost in his own thoughts.

Still mourning his friend. His lover? Who knows. He sure won't tell me. There's a human being under all that macho crap. It doesn't come out much, though.

"They asked if I knew about a cave," Jana said.

Jacob nodded. "They asked me the same thing. I lied and told them it was on one of the islands, and they told me that was the wrong answer. I was trying to be taken prisoner, but I guess they saw right through me and left me down there."

"When I came up for air the second time, I noticed their ship heading south. There's nothing between the islands and the shore in that direction, so I guess they were heading for the coast."

Jacob thought for a moment. "So, maybe they think this cave has all the loot from the *Santo Santiago*?"

"Maybe. Maybe they have a second treasure map, one we don't know about."

Jacob mulled this over, then called over his shoulder to Eva. "Are there a lot of cliffs along this stretch of coastline?"

"Not where we are now, but if you head south-southwest from the islands, you'll come to an area with a lot of cliffs. There might be sea caves there."

"You were listening to our conversation?" Jacob said. "I thought teenagers never listened to adults."

"Stop trying to be funny. You suck at it."

Jacob grinned.

"We need to find out if there's a sea cave in the region," Jana said. "Eva, do any of your dad's charts detail the geology of the shore?"

"No. I've studied all those charts. They don't show caves. But they're nautical charts. Maybe they didn't bother to include them."

Eva brought over a steaming plate of ramen, which Jana started to devour. She had eaten way too much ramen in her broke university days and hadn't touched it since, but she was famished and didn't even taste it as she shoveled it down.

Jacob, between mouthfuls of his own plate of ramen, said, "They wouldn't have asked us if they knew where it was. Maybe their second treasure map is vague as to its location. Seems strange it wouldn't be on a modern map."

"Erosion, dummy," Eva said.

"Huh?"

"Sea cliffs erode. You know? Wind? Waves? The entrance probably got covered up like ages ago."

He looked at Jana, who rolled her eyes and said, "Yeah, Jacob, that's like totally obvious."

"Totally," Eva agreed. The girl fetched a bucket and started scooping up water from the cargo hold, walked to the stern, and dumped it over the side.

"Well, if it's covered up, how the hell do we find it?" Jacob asked.

"Good question. At least if it's hard for us, it will be hard for the pirates, too," Jana said.

She thought for a moment, an old memory tugging at her mind. Something Brian had mentioned right at the beginning of the dig.

Poor Brian. He had signed up for an excavation, then signed up for a date with her, and nearly got killed. She was turning into someone like Jacob, endangering the lives of everyone around her.

Damn it, what was it he had said? Something about Venezuela ...

She snapped her fingers. "The coastal survey!"

"The what?"

"Brian. Um, one of my colleagues."

"The guy that got kidnapped?"

"Yeah."

More than a colleague, then.

"Oh."

"He mentioned that he'd been offered work on a coastal survey around the Caribbean. A professor at his university is studying land and maritime use by prehistoric peoples around the Caribbean. He's working with geologists and oceanographers to survey the entire coastline to look for potential archaeological sites."

"You think they might have found the cave?"

"Maybe, maybe not. But they'd look for potential cave sites. Those yield the best-preserved prehistoric remains."

"That's nice, but let me remind you that we're wounded, in a foundering boat, and out of touch with your friend. How are we supposed to get our hands on some archaeological survey published in the United States?"

Jana smiled. "Leave that to me."

***

It was evening by the time they reached a private pier of one of Néstor's dubious friends.

It lay in a tiny little cove the *Searunner* could barely squeeze into. Flanked by two rocky peninsulas that all but hid it from view, the entrance led to a small, almost round body of water a quarter mile

125

across. Two boats, a sailboat and a speedboat, were moored to a pier. Behind it stood a large, wooden bungalow, and behind that a dark line of trees.

Jana, standing at the prow and feeling much better after a few hours of loving care by a very strange teenager, could barely make any of this out. Only a couple of dim lights shone on the pier to guide Néstor, and no lights shone at all in the bungalow.

What she could see from the lights on the pier was a fat man in a t-shirt, shorts, and a bucket hat standing on the end of the pier, a Kalashnikov in one hand and a beer can in the other.

"Well look what the cat dragged in," the man said in Spanish with a Venezuelan accent. "Damn, you guys look like you've been in a fight. Was it with the Coast Guard? If it was, the mooring fee's doubled."

"Hi, Mauricio," Eva said. "It was pirates."

"Bad news. Bet you gave them a bloody nose, though."

"We did," the teenager said, tossing him the mooring rope.

Mauricio tossed his beer can into the water, grabbed the rope, and tied it to the bollard.

He peered at Jana, and then at Jacob, who was just coming out of the cabin.

"And who are these two?"

"None of your business," Jana said.

"Fair enough. You guys want dinner? I was just cooking up some steaks."

Jana and Jacob's stomachs rumbled in unison. That sounded a lot better than ramen.

"Dad, you're paying for dinner," Eva called over her shoulder.

"Why me?" Néstor called back from the pilot's cabin.

"The pirates took their wallets, remember?"

Our passports too. That's going to be a problem. We're in Venezuela with no ID and no visa.

"Did you see what happened to our ship? The money we got paid won't even begin to cover it."

"Too bad. You're buying them dinner."

"Fine," Néstor grumbled.

Eva turned to Jana. "Nothing's for free with Mauricio. He's a pig."

"Yes, and your father is a noble, upright citizen," Mauricio said. "Secure that mess you call a boat and I'll get to work on the steaks. Come on into the dining room when you're done, Eva. You know the way."

Mauricio thumped off down the pier. Eva stuck her tongue out at him.

"Is he safe?" Jana whispered to her.

"Safe as long as you pay him," the girl whispered back.

"How much does it cost to use the phone?" Jana asked.

"Lots." She called over her shoulder. "Dad, we're going to the shop!"

"Ugh. Why do you always spend my money?"

"I'm your kid. It's my job to spend your money."

"Oh, yeah."

"Come on," Eva said.

She led Jana and Jacob down the pier and around the side of the bungalow to a door. Jana looked around and couldn't see much beyond a narrow yard and the dark woods beyond. The girl seemed to know her way, though, as she opened the door and flicked a light switch inside.

They found themselves in a small shop. Provisions, camping gear, and boat supplies filled shelves to either side. A glass counter displaying electronics ran along the opposite wall, and beyond an open door behind it, they could see Mauricio standing at a grill with several steaks sizzling on it. The smell nearly made Jana vault over the counter and grab one.

"Dinner will be up in a few minutes," he called through the doorway. "Need something from the store?"

Jana noticed that inside the glass counter were a number of burner phones, as well as walkie-talkies, a couple of powerful shortwave transceivers, and a satellite phone.

"Do the burner phones have enough credit to call internationally?" Jana said.

"Sure. Talk with your girlfriends all you want."

"I'll take one. You got any weapons?"

"Nope. Can't sell guns," Mauricio said, flipping the steaks with a dirty spatula. "It's against the rules."

Jacob snorted. "Like you don't ever break the law."

"I didn't say it was against the law. I said it's against the rules. Rule around here is that only one man can sell guns, and he lives over in the next town. I'd send you his way, but he's out of town at the moment doing I-don't-want-to-know-what."

"So, no guns," Jacob said, crestfallen.

"No guns." Mauricio passed through the door and stood behind the counter. Jana saw he had put on a stained apron and had a greasy face

127

with heavy jowls. His arms looked powerful, though, and Jana got the impression he could more than hold his own in a fight.

"Just the burner then," Jana said.

"I take cash or trade," Mauricio said with a grin that showed a gold front tooth.

"I told you he was a pig," Eva said.

"He better not talk to you like that," Jana replied.

"He doesn't have the guts."

"I got plenty of guts!" Mauricio said with a laugh, slapping his belly.

"Give her the burner and stop being a dork."

"She got money? She looks like you fished her out of the sea."

"My dad's paying for it."

Jacob turned to her. "I'll talk to my superiors and see that you're compensated for everything."

Eva rolled her eyes. "That's what you said about the sharks."

Mauricio guffawed, pointing at Jacob. "That was him? Mother of God, you're a serious screwup, my friend!"

Mauricio and Eva laughed as Jacob stood there blushing. Jana took the burner phone and stepped outside.

For a moment, she stood in the darkness, the only sounds were the crickets in the woods and the half-heard conversation inside. She stared at the phone, her heart beginning to beat faster. She hadn't talked to Brian Tanner since she had left for Europe. She had left behind an uncertain relationship, one awkward night out, and a kidnapping by persons unknown. And now she had to call him out of the blue and ask him to do some research for her?

At least she had his number. In an email, she had an attachment with a list of all the workers on the excavation and their contact information. She turned on the phone, accessed her email, and found his number.

She paused again. Would he even answer? It was late enough here that it would be early morning in Morocco, assuming he was still in Morocco. Had the Moroccan secret service there sent him on a plane to the United States already, as they had promised?

That had only been a couple of days ago. It seemed like a couple of years.

Probably, he was still in Morocco. If he was in the States, then it wasn't too late, so he might still be up.

If he was en route, then they had no way of finding the caves. It was a slim hope anyway.

Jana realized she was delaying. She forced herself to dial the number.

It picked up on the third ring.

"Hello?" Brian's voice sounded guarded. After what he'd been through, a call from an unidentified number would seem like a threat.

"Hi Brian, it's Jana."

"Jana! Thank God you're all right." Pause. "You're all right, aren't you? You sound different."

"Just tired. Where are you?"

"Still in Morocco. I'm flying out tomorrow. So, what's going on? They're telling me you're being targeted by terrorists for that mosaic we dug up."

Brian didn't sound like he believed that story.

"Look, Brian, I need your help. Remember that Caribbean survey you told me about? The one your professor wanted you to go on?"

"Huh?"

"Did they publish a geological map of the Venezuelan coast?"

"Huh?"

"Brian, I know this is an odd request, and I'm afraid I can't explain, but I need a detailed geological map of the Venezuelan coast, preferably one done recently and to a fine scale. Can you get me one?"

"What the hell? You keep vanishing, some psycho nearly kills me trying to get to you, and then you call me on a different phone asking me for … what exactly?"

"A geological map of the Venezuelan coast, preferably one with an older map for comparison."

"What are you doing in Venezuela?"

Jana couldn't help but smile. He was catching up.

"I can't talk about that. Did your professor make that kind of map?"

"Yeah. What's going on?"

"Could you get me that map?"

"Are you in trouble? Should I come down there?"

Jana's heart skipped a beat. "No! Don't come down!"

Pause. "So, you are in trouble."

"I'm sorry, Brian, but I can't explain. We just really need that map."

"We?"

Oh, crap.

"Me and a colleague." *That makes it sound like you're a spy.* "Me and a friend."

"What have you got yourself into?"

If I told you, you wouldn't believe me. "I can't talk about that now."

"Has it got something to do with your disappearances during the dig? And the attempt on your life? Should I inform the embassy and get you out of there?"

"No! Jesus Christ, Brian, could you just get us the damn map?"

Another pause, longer this time. Jana realized she had taken it a step too far. After all he'd been through, poor Brian had every reason to hang up on her.

"All right," he said at last. "I'll get you the map. I'll get you the entire survey and email it to you. But I want an explanation after you've done whatever it is you're doing."

Jana felt a brief annoyance at the possessiveness in his tone, then reminded herself that he had nearly been killed because of her. He deserved some sort of explanation.

Just what that would be, she had no idea.

First, she had to study the map and, assuming they could get a lead on the cave, get there before the pirates.

And hopefully stop them, even though they didn't have any weapons.

CHAPTER TWENTY

Jacob and the others stared at Mauricio's computer screen in his mess of an office as Jana scrolled through the report her colleague had sent her. It was a long PDF document filled with charts and diagrams.

"Using the computer isn't free, you know," Mauricio said, sipping a beer.

"Of course not," Jacob grumbled.

"And if you want to print something—"

"Yeah, yeah."

"Here's the section on Venezuela," Jana announced.

She scrolled through a mass of text until she got to a detailed geological map of the coastline.

"Bingo," Jacob said.

"What's that mean?" Eva asked.

"Bingo is a game. If you win, you shout out 'Bingo!'"

"Sounds like a boring game for old people."

Jacob grinned. "As a matter of fact, it is."

They all studied the map, Jana zooming in to the section near their location where the beaches gave way to steep cliffs.

"I'm not seeing any caves," Néstor said.

"Neither am I," Jana replied. "Let's see what other illustrations they have. After that, I'll read the text."

"Glad you're doing it," Eva said. "Looks boring."

"Archaeology isn't boring," Jana said. "Especially not lately."

She scrolled to the next page and took in a sharp breath.

Taking up the whole page was a reproduction of an old nautical chart of the same stretch of coastline. The caption said the map was from 1802. A large sea cave was clearly marked on it.

"Whoa," Eva said. "Cool."

Jana turned to her and smiled. "I told you archaeology isn't boring."

She zoomed in on the cave. The map was fairly detailed for the period and showed numerous rocks off the shore as well as some dangerously shallow portions.

Néstor pointed to a spot out at sea and traced a line along the deeper portions of water to the mouth of the cave. "That's a rough approach, but a good sailor could make it as long as the seas were calm."

"Is that big enough for a pirate ship?" Jacob asked.

"Maybe. How big was the *Vengeance*?"

"We're not sure," Jana answered. "Probably frigate sized, like the *Santo Santiago*. Pirates wanted smaller, faster ships that could outmaneuver pursuits in shallow and dangerous waters."

"An old-style frigate could get in there," the captain said.

Jana scrolled back to look at the modern survey map, then switched back and forth between the two pages trying to compare the old coastline to the new one.

"It would be easier if we printed those pages out," Jacob said.

"There's a charge for that," Mauricio said.

"Of course there is," Jacob grumbled.

"You're such a dork, and why does this place smell like old socks?"

"Probably because of those old socks over there," Mauricio said, pointing to a pile of socks under a nearby desk.

"Eeew. I'm going outside."

They printed the pages, Mauricio adding the amount to a tally he kept in a little notebook he carried in his pocket. Jana set the two charts side by side on the desk right above the socks.

Brave woman, Jacob thought, hanging back a bit.

She and Néstor studied the charts for a moment.

"There!" they said at the same time, putting their fingers down on the same spot. On the new chart, no cave appeared.

"So, it really did get covered up by a landslide," Mauricio said. "Do you think that pirate ship is still in there?"

Jana gave him a hard look. "Our discovery, our ship."

"My country," Mauricio grunted. "But if you want me to stay away, that's going to cost you. Say a hundred dollars a day?"

Jacob resisted the urge to slap him.

Jana went back to the computer and scanned through the accompanying text.

"There's no mention of the field crew finding the cave."

"In that case, 200 dollars a day," Mauricio said. He picked up the modern map and belched. "No way Néstor is going to be able to sail you up to that cliff. The *Searunner* can barely maneuver. I don't want to risk any of my boats either. There's a road along that stretch that will get you close. You'll only have to hike a kilometer through the jungle to get to the clifftop. I'll drive you there in the morning."

"For a price," Jacob said.

Mauricio grinned, showing off his gold front tooth. "You're learning."

***

They got to the clifftop just as the sun peeked over the eastern horizon. The jungle reached right to the edge, and from its cover, they peered through the leaves and vines out at the stunning view of the sparkling water and the waves crashing into the rocks jutting from the sea close to shore.

Jacob scanned the area for any ships. He saw a small sailboat, a simple pleasure craft that couldn't carry more than two people, about half a mile out. A couple of tankers were on the horizon. Nothing more.

Good.

They moved to the edge of the cliff and looked down.

Jacob did not like what he saw.

The cliff plunged almost sheer to the surf-lashed rocks fifty feet below. While the cliff face was jagged, offering lots of handholds and footholds, the rock looked eroded and friable, ready to snap off if too much weight was put on it.

This was going to be a dangerous climb, especially with his right wrist still hurting. That pirate had given it a nasty twist underwater and trying to swim to shore sure didn't help the healing process.

He remembered a time when he and Aaron had been doing a forced march through the desert in southern Algeria. They had to make a rendezvous with a people smuggler who would get them across the border into Niger, where they could find shelter at a French Foreign Legion outpost. Jacob had sprained his ankle in a firefight and was lagging behind, each mile adding to the torture. The people smuggler, who had gotten them into the country and made Mauricio seem as innocent as a church organist, had told them that if they were late, he'd leave them.

"I know you're in pain," said the man who had become a father figure to him. "But you'll be in a lot more pain if you fail."

It wasn't some macho threat, simply a statement of fact. Jacob had gritted his teeth and increased his pace. They made it to the rendezvous.

"Let's get climbing," Jacob said to the woman at his side. "You remember how I showed you how to tie in?"

"Yeah. I'll go first," Jana said.

"No, I'll go first. You can see how I do it. Plus, my wrist is killing me and if I slip, I don't want to take you with me."

Something he had learned in his Ranger training. Never hide a weakness from your team. They needed to know.

"All right," Jana said, giving him a concerned look.

Mauricio had provided them with two small pickaxes like prospectors used and a length of rope. For a price, of course. Jacob owed Néstor a lot of money. Jana unwound the rope and tied it around the trunk of a nearby tree.

"You sure we're right above it?" Jacob asked.

"As close as I can determine. So no, probably not."

"Only one way to find out."

Jacob wrapped the rope around him in a simple rappelling method. He wished he had a harness, but Mauricio didn't have any available and didn't know where to get any. You could rappel without one, but it wasn't as safe, and you needed to exert more effort with your hands, exactly what Jacob didn't want to do.

But he had no choice, so he did it.

He leaned back until the rope was taut and began to rappel down the slope. Since it wasn't perfectly vertical, he descended the slope in a sort of half-walk, using his feet as much as possible while the rope held much of his weight.

Even so, he only got about five feet down before a rock snapped off under his foot. He jerked down, his wrist flashing with pain as he scrambled with his feet to find purchase again.

"You OK?" Jana called down. She was on her hands and knees looking over the cliff.

"Oh, yeah. Just super."

"Sarcasm sounds better coming from Eva."

"Stop being a dork and make sure that rope is still secure on the tree."

"Very funny." Her head disappeared. "Yeah, it is."

Jacob continued his descent, looking to his left and right for any fissure in the rock that might lead to the cave. It was possible the entrance was completely covered up. If so, then at least the pirates couldn't get in either.

Back at Mauricio's place, he had briefly considered calling Arnold Reece, the field office director in Caracas. Then he realized that with his undermanned team stretched to the limit, Reece couldn't spare any backup for what still seemed like a wild goose chase. Sure, the pirates existed, but could the original *Vengeance* still really exist? Or Ulloa's glass sphere full of a centuries-old virus?

And he couldn't call the Venezuelan authorities either. While they would try to catch the pirates and seal off the area around the cave, he and Jana wouldn't be able to go in there themselves.

And if there was anything Jacob Snow had learned over the years, it was that he would much rather rely on himself and his team than some local police in a country where they were regularly bought.

So here he was, rappelling with insufficient gear down a treacherous cliff above jagged rocks and rough surf when he should be recovering at home in bed.

He kept going, his wrist throbbing, placing his feet with care, sweat breaking out on his brow despite the sea breeze only just beginning to grow warm in the rising sun, until he was more than halfway down to the water.

Then something caught his eye.

A few yards to his right was a dark fissure about half the height of a man and barely wide enough to squeeze into. Could that be it?

He sidestepped toward it. When he got about halfway there, his rope yanked at him, causing a twinge of pain in his already aching wrist.

He looked up and saw it was caught on an outcropping.

Jacob took a step back to his left to give it some slack and whipped the rope, trying to loosen it from the stones catching it.

That loosened more than the rope. It sent a cascade of small stones bouncing down the steep slope at him.

Cursing, he tried to dodge them all. He avoided the big ones, but a couple of smaller stones, half the size of baseballs, hit his shoulder and chest.

Jana's head appeared over him again.

"You OK?"

"Ow. Sort of. I think I found something."

"I can't see anything from up here."

"Good. Maybe that means it's undisturbed, assuming it's actually an entrance. Looks deep, though. I can't see the end."

He moved over to the fissure, aware that if he slipped now, he would swing to the left like a pendulum, bashing himself against the face of the cliff.

Luckily, he didn't and managed to get the bottom half of his body into a tight jam in the rock. Doing so set off another cascade of smaller stones, but the main section of cliff held.

Jacob peered between his feet and saw a tunnel leading down.

He flicked on the light strapped to his forehead (purchased from Mauricio at an inflated price) and looked again.

The tunnel twisted out of sight just a few feet beyond him.

"Of course it wouldn't be that easy," he grumbled.

He untethered himself, wrapped the end of the rope around a stone jutting out nearby, and crawled into the narrow space.

At first the way tightened, and he didn't think he could make it through, but with a bit of squirming and grunting, his burned skin scraping painfully against the rough rock, he came to a wider portion that wasn't so steep. There he was able to turn around and go headfirst.

After a few more feet of crawling, the way opened up.

And what he saw made him scramble back up to the entrance.

"Jana! Get down here! You won't believe it!"

CHAPTER TWENTY ONE

Jana stared and stared. And stared some more. Jacob had been right. She couldn't believe she was seeing what she was actually seeing.

Through the light of their combined headlamps, they beheld a vast sea cave, running so deep into the cliff that the back was lost in darkness.

But between them and the back of the cave sat something Jana had never thought she'd come across in all of her explorations of the past.

A complete sailing ship from the eighteenth century.

It sat on the rocky floor of the cave, no trace of water around it. The avalanche that had sealed the cave must have sealed off the sea as well, and the water trapped inside must have drained off into some unseen fissure in the floor.

What remained was the crumpled remains of a pirate ship. The keel and lower portions of the hull had deteriorated somewhat, buckling under the weight of the middle and upper decks so that it was now a third of its original height. That gave the surreal impression that the *Vengeance* was sailing through the stone.

The top deck looked remarkably preserved, with cannons and masts still in place. The sails were mere shreds of canvas hanging from the mast, but much of the rigging remained still. The ship had raised fore and aft decks.

The tunnel they had come through took them to one side and a bit above the floor, giving them a perfect view of the best-preserved premodern ship ever to be found.

And she had helped find it.

This was a career-making discovery, something far better than the mosaic back in Morocco. This was iconic, something that would get on the cover of *National Geographic*, get on every television channel. This was on par with the discovery of Tutankhamun's tomb.

Her thoughts must have made it to her face because Jacob nudged her. "Hey. Remember what we're here for."

"Oh, right."

"How could it be so well preserved after all this time?"

"It's sheltered from the elements. Plus, do you see that sparkle on the walls?"

"Yeah, it's kind of creepy looking."

"Salt. That mixed with the natural humidity in the air seems to have created a balance where the wood doesn't rot due to damp or dry out too much. You can see the lower portions got too much damp before the water drained out. That's why they rotted and buckled."

"Amazing. Let's get down there."

The side of the cave was shaped like a crescent, with rough stones on the lower portion. They found it relatively easy to climb down to the bottom and come level with the base of the ship.

For a moment, they stood and stared, their headlamps illuminating the ship more clearly. The gun ports of the middle deck were all open, with the muzzles of the cannons pointing out. Here and there, she spotted damage from the fight it had with the *Santo Santiago*, patched up with boards to keep out the elements.

Jacob pointed at an open gun port on the middle deck. For some reason, there was no cannon blocking it. Just below it was a heap of broken and partially rotted timbers. "I think we can get in there."

Jana went first. No way was she going second with a find like this.

She clambered up the heap of wood that was all that remained of the lower hold, wincing a couple of times when boards snapped off beneath her feet. She grasped the bottom of the gun port and lifted herself up.

The first thing she saw was the muzzle of the cannon, set a bit back from its gun port as if it had been fired, but not reloaded, and replaced in position. She moved her head to the left and right, scanning the interior of the middle deck.

Her skin crawled at what she saw. A perfect interior of guns and other equipment. Kegs of gunpowder, a water barrel, a lantern still hanging from a hook on one of the beams, and in between the cannons, a scattering of human skeletons, still wearing their clothing, victims of the Black Fever.

"It couldn't still be in the air, could it?" she whispered. She felt like she was in a mausoleum. In a way, she was.

"No. Not after all this time," Jacob said, whispering too. "If it was that strong, it would have wiped out the world's population."

Feeling only partially reassured, she crawled through the gun port. As she set her foot down, she heard and felt something crunch underfoot.

She withdrew her foot and saw the crushed remains of a rat skeleton. Looking around again, she noticed smaller skeletons scattered amid the human ones.

"It killed the rats too."

"Maybe the rats died after they ran out of food."

Food.

She studied the nearest skeleton, still wearing its loose pants and white shirt with a red bandanna around its skull and a wide belt of black leather with a brass buckle around its waist.

The clothing was rotted with age, but Jana could discern places where the cloth had been chewed through.

Jana shuddered.

She stepped into the pirate ship, the first living thing to do so for more than 200 years. The boards creaked ominously underfoot. Jacob climbed up behind her and looked around, openmouthed with wonder.

"We have to watch our step. Some of the boards are rotten," she told him.

In a few spots, the cannons had cracked through the deck, and sat at crazy angles, part of their bases in the holes. In a couple of spots, they had broken right through, leaving gaping spaces.

Jana moved as close as she dared to one of these and looked down.

The cannon lay on a pile of crushed chests, gold doubloons shining through the splintered wood. Jana's heart skipped a beat.

Archaeologists always said they searched for knowledge, not treasure, but finding treasure was nice too.

She felt a poke in her side.

"We're here for something else," Jacob said.

Jana let out a gust of breath. "Right."

They looked around at the skeletons and cannons. A cutlass lay nearby, and not far beyond that was a flintlock pistol.

"There's so much here, where do we start?" Jana asked.

"You said Ulloa put the glass sphere into a small, padded chest. The pirates would have thought this was something unusual. They might have interrogated Ulloa and discovered what it was, or they might have simply looted it. Either way, they would probably keep it somewhere special. I'm thinking the captain's quarters."

"And where would that be? I'm a Roman specialist, not a pirate fan."

Jacob grinned, teeth white in the circle of Jana's light. "And I'm a guy who read lots of pirate books as a kid. Follow me."

He led her to a set of stairs leading up to the main deck. He went first, nearly falling as one of the treads snapped under his weight.

"Careful!"

"If I wanted to be careful, I would have never joined the CIA."

They managed to get up the rest of the steps without any trouble and found themselves on deck. Not far off lay a dozen skeletons in a circle, several empty bottles of rum scattered around them along with some clay pipes. Each man had a flintlock pistol in his hand, and each skull had a hole in the temple.

Jana's heart sank.

"They knew they were dying. They had one last party and then shot themselves."

"Poor bastards," Jacob muttered. "I know they were bloodthirsty criminals, but what a horrible way to go."

He pointed to the raised back of the ship. "That's the aftcastle. The raised section on the prow is the forecastle. The captain usually had his quarters in the aftcastle. It was roomier and more sheltered from the wind." He nudged her with his elbow and grinned. "Oh, and you know what the deck on top of the aftcastle is called? The poop deck! Hee hee. That always gave me the giggles."

Jana rolled her eyes. "Now I know why you get along so well with children. You are one."

Jacob shrugged and moved over to the aftcastle. A closed door with a brass handle led inside. Jacob reached for the handle, paused, and let out a little shiver.

Despite all his bluster, he's in awe of this place too.

He turned the handle. The door opened with a loud creak that echoed through the darkened sea cave.

Inside, they saw a rectangular room with a low beamed ceiling. To their left stood a table covered with navigational charts, a sextant, and a telescope. To their right was a narrow bed. On the bed lay a skeleton in a buff coat and loose pants. The skull had a patch over one eye socket. A tricorn hat hung from the bedpost. On the bedside table were two empty bottles of wine and a glass made of the finest crystal.

For a moment, they simply looked at the dead captain in silence.

"No pistol," Jana whispered. "He fought until the end."

Jana spotted a large wooden sea chest at the base of the bed. Moving over to it, she opened it up.

Inside, she found a change of clothing, a leather bag that, from the way it bulged, probably contained coins and jewels, and a small, wooden chest.

"Whoa," Jacob said.

"My feelings exactly."

"Be careful."

"Oh, I will be. Trust me."

"I do trust you."

The subtle force of this statement made her look at him. He gave a nod, and she turned back to the chest.

There was a lock, but the key was in it. Gently, she turned it until she heard a soft click and then opened the lid.

The interior was entirely filled with purple velvet, the lid similarly padded.

Sitting in the center was a glass sphere the size of a softball. Inside the sphere was a small bit of flesh.

"What's that?" Jacob asked.

"Looks like some sort of gland. The sources didn't mention this. Ulloa must have put a gland from one of the patients inside the sphere as well as the concentrated breath of those dying of Black Fever."

"So, the air is concentrated in there? That means if it breaks, the contagion will shoot out like shrapnel from a grenade."

"But far deadlier."

Jana closed the lid and, with infinite care, lifted the casket out of the sea chest.

"Once we get back to Mauricio's, we need to call your boss in Caracas. Secure this site from treasure hunters."

"All right, but first we need to secure this glass thing."

"Agreed."

As much as she wanted to explore this nautical time capsule all day, she knew that getting Ulloa's sphere to a safe place was the far bigger priority.

They walked out of the aftcastle, and suddenly got blinded as half a dozen lights turned on and shined at them.

From beyond the glare, someone laughed.

"Look, it's the two Americans again. And I think they have just what we came for, boys."

141

CHAPTER TWENTY TWO

Jacob recognized the voice in an instant. It was the pirate captain. Him and his crew had either followed them here or figured out the location for themselves.

"Hand over that casket. You have six guns trained on you."

Jacob paused. He had no weapons except for a prospector's pick hanging from his belt.

"How did you find us?" he asked, playing for time.

"We spotted your rope. Hand over that casket."

Thinking quickly, he said, "This casket is full of jewels. Diamonds, rubies, emeralds. It's worth a fortune. It's yours if you just let us go."

"Jewels?" the captain said, sounding confused.

"Yeah, look." Jacob flipped open the lid and grabbed the sphere, holding it in front of them like a cross to ward off a vampire. "Go ahead and shoot. If you hit this sphere, it will explode and all of you will die."

The lights moved back a little as each pirate tried to increase the distance between himself and the mysterious orb. Obviously, the captain had shared with his crew just what it was they were hunting for.

"You'll die, too," the captain said, sounding unsure of himself for the first time.

"If we give this up, you'll kill us. Our only chance is to hold this glass sphere for ransom and use it to get out of here."

A low chuckle came from the captain. "I like you, American. You got style. Guts too. But who are you, really? You're no drug runner."

Jacob tossed the sphere from one hand to the other, making everyone gasp, including Jana.

"No, I'm not a drug runner. I'm something that can cause far worse trouble for you. So, I suggest you back off and let us out. You lost, whatever your name is, but you won. All we want is the sphere. The ship and all its plunder are yours if you just let us go."

"This is a trick," another pirate said. "He's with the police."

"Maybe," the captain replied. "I'm not sure we have much choice. All right, American. You win. For the moment. Take the sphere and go."

"I'm sure you have someone at the cave entrance, and more on top of the cliff. One of your men will have to leave his weapons and come with us as a hostage."

A pirate laughed. "One of us as a hostage! You don't seem to realize the situation you're in. You're outnumbered and defenseless!"

"Defenseless?" Jacob started juggling the orb, making everyone squirm with fear. He wanted to squirm, too, but he had to focus on juggling. His wrist still hurt. Good thing Ulloa's weird creation wasn't too heavy.

"Stop that!" the captain said. "All right, all right. Frederico, go with them."

"Why me?" one of the pirates asked.

"Because I said so!"

Jacob stopped juggling. Everyone let out a breath of relief. Jacob did too. He hoped nobody heard. One of the pirates laid down his shotgun and stepped forward, glaring at Jacob.

"You pull anything, and I'll kill you with my bare hands," Frederico said.

He spoke with a Mexican accent. That sparked a memory in Jacob that he didn't have time to mull over. He had to survive the next five minutes first.

"All right," Jacob said, trying to sound more confident than he felt. "We're going to those stairs over there that go below decks. There's a gun port that gives easy access out. You probably came in that way. The lady goes first, then me, and then you."

Frederico nodded.

They moved toward the stairs. Just as they made it, Frederico leapt forward and grabbed the sphere. Jacob tried to pull back, and it slipped from both of their grasps.

Jacob fumbled, tried to grab it, but Frederico's hands got in the way. He watched, as if in slow motion, as the sphere fell toward the hard, wooden deck.

Jana dove in and caught it.

She grunted as she landed hard on her elbows and yet managed to keep hold of the sphere.

Jacob slugged Frederico, using his off hand, his uninjured hand, but connecting solidly enough that the pirate staggered to the side.

Another pirate ducked in, and Jacob landed a kick in his midsection that doubled him over and sent him flying back. Jana struggled to her feet.

"Don't shoot!" the pirate captain shouted. "Nobody shoot! We can't risk it!"

They didn't shoot, but that didn't stop them from attacking. The captain came at Jana, arms wide for a tackle, while two of his men attacked Jacob from opposite directions.

Jacob dropped to the deck, swept the feet out from under one pirate, and made him fall against his comrade, headbutting him on the way down.

That made the second guy fall too. Jacob sprang to his feet and saw that Jana had slipped away from the captain's grasp and was running in a zigzag around the deck, being chased by the captain and the one pirate that remained standing.

Two more were getting up.

Jana ran toward the stairs leading up to the forecastle, but the captain cut her off, and the other pirate closed in from behind.

"Jana!" Jacob shouted.

Jana saw she was about to get caught and did something that made everybody holler.

She tossed the orb to Jacob.

It sailed over the deck, followed by everyone's headlamps. Jacob caught it with both hands.

The next instant, he had to duck to the side as Frederico tried to grab him.

He had to duck again as another pirate approached and retreated toward the aftdeck.

A pirate got between him and the cabin door, so Jacob ducked to the right and hurried up the steps to the poop deck, praying none of the old boards snapped under his feet.

They didn't. He got to the poop deck safely, swinging around to check on the others. The deck of the pirate ship looked like a disco with all the lights swinging around. One pirate was coming up the steps behind him, while another angled over to come up another set of stairs to the poop deck on the starboard side. A pirate was still down thanks to the headbutt inadvertently given to him by a comrade, and the headbutter was just beginning to rise. Jana and a pirate were struggling close to the forecastle while the captain was rushing aftwards, toward Jacob.

Jacob saw a cutlass lying on the poop deck nearby. He grabbed it and, with a flourish, swung it at the head of the man ascending the steps ahead of him.

While the guy obeyed his captain's order not to fire, he still had a rifle in his hands. He brought it up to parry the blow.

Jacob had grabbed the cutlass with his injured right hand, not daring to entrust the glass sphere to a hand that was so weakened. The jarring impact of the cutlass on the steel barrel of the rifle sent a shockwave of pain through his wrist and made him drop the blade.

Luckily, the pirate dodged back as the blow landed, and that made him misjudge his step. He fell head over heels back down the stairs.

The captain leapt over him and came up the stairs, a large knife gleaming in the bobbing light of his headlamp. The pirate coming up the other set of stairs had made it to the poop deck and was closing in.

Jacob spotted a rope tied to a nearby railing, running up to somewhere out of sight on the central mast. Daring to put the orb in his injured hand, he used his good hand to unwind the rope, jumped onto the railing, and swung over the length of the main deck.

"Huzzah!" he shouted as he sailed over the heads of the pirates.

He always wanted to shout that on a pirate ship, ever since he was six. If he was going to die in the next few seconds, now was the time.

There was the snap of wood overhead, and suddenly, he wasn't swinging forward but falling down.

"Yikes!"

He grasped the orb with both hands just in time not to drop it when he landed hard on his back.

As luck would have it, he landed on a rotted part of the deck, and smacked right through, leaving a Jacob-sized hole in a priceless maritime artifact.

Jana's going to kill me.

He lay there, stunned for a few crucial seconds as he heard the sound of running feet upstairs. Then he heard them on the steps coming down.

Wavering lights appeared in the middle deck, focusing on him. He struggled to rise and saw he had landed right on top of a pirate skeleton, pulverizing it.

"Yuck. Sorry, buddy."

The pirates closed in. Jacob stepped back and stumbled. He had been running on empty for too long, had never recovered from the bombing incident, and now he could barely stay upright, let alone fight or run.

"Jacob!" Jana's voice called from above him.

He looked up through the hole, saw Jana standing at the edge of it looking down at him, and tossed the orb up to her. She caught it and disappeared out of sight.

Jacob turned to face the pirates, ready to delay them as long as possible, and got a rifle butt right in the forehead.

He blacked out.

CHAPTER TWENTY THREE

Jana ran for the railing, hoping to leap over it and away, but barely got three steps before the cold muzzle of a pistol jabbed against the base of her skull.

"Don't move," Frederico ordered.

Jana froze. Another pirate came up and took the orb from her.

"Mounir! We got it!" Frederico shouted.

The two pirates moved away a little, the Mexican still covering her with his pistol.

The pirate captain came back up from the middle deck.

"You got it?"

"Yeah."

The two pirates turned away from her at the same time, showing their captain their prize. Jana switched off her headlamp and vaulted over the railing.

"Get her!"

Jana landed hard on the stone floor of the cave. She stumbled, caught her footing, and ran away from the ship. She stumbled again two steps later, nearly falling when she banged her shin against a large stone.

Three headlamps appeared at the railing, swinging back and forth, seeking her out.

They gave her light to see by, and she picked up speed over the cave's rough floor, moving farther into its hidden recesses.

One of the beams focused on her.

"There she is!"

A deafening burst of fire echoed through the cave. Bullets panged off the rocks all around her. Jana had nowhere to hide.

She jerked her body, forced all her muscles to relax, and fell hard on the ground, curled up at an awkward angle. Her head and shoulder throbbed from where they had impacted against the stone. She waited, keeping totally still, face pressed against the ground, not daring to breathe.

"Got her!"

If they decide to double tap me, I'm gone.

Silence. Jana dared a peek. She could see lights moving about on deck, and more passing by the gun ports on the middle deck.

"What about all this?" someone called in Arabic.

The captain replied in the same language, but with a Berber accent, "Grab what you can. We're leaving in two minutes."

Jana stayed where she was, terrified and despondent. They had failed. The pirates had Ulloa's sphere, and they had Jacob. She was unarmed and alone.

"Remember, as long as you're alive, you can fight."

That's what Dad always used to say. But how the hell was she supposed to fight?

She'd find a way. The stakes were too high to give up.

Jana watched as the pirates, laughing, and joking among themselves, moved around the ship, especially the middle deck and captain's quarters. She snarled with impotent fury to see these thugs plundering a priceless archaeological site.

Then she saw something that caused her to feel a very different emotion—fear.

The yellow, wavering light of flames.

They came from the porthole of the aftdeck. After a moment, she saw them on the foredeck too.

They were burning the ship, with Jacob still inside!

The pirates moved off toward the cave entrance, still laughing, six lights like evil spirits heading up to haunt the surface world.

Jana began to crawl forward, worried they might hear. She had to get to Jacob, assuming they hadn't slit his throat.

One by one the pirates' lights disappeared into the crawlspace leading to the cliff. Jana, her nostrils already stinging from smoke, climbed up the side of the ship to a gun port and squeezed around the cannon.

Smoke curled along the ceiling of the middle deck and hung in a heavy haze all around, lit by the garish flames springing up from a pile of old sacks that had probably once contained grain. Jacob lay moaning on the floor, rubbing a bloody bump on his forehead, barely conscious.

"Jacob? Jacob!" Jana rushed over and lifted him up into a sitting position.

"Ugh. Jana?" his voice sounded weak, distant.

"Jacob, get up. We need to go."

She dragged him over to the gun port they had entered, the one where the cannon was set back and gave them more room. The flames suddenly grew brighter. She glanced over and saw a terrible sight. One of the dead pirates, his clothing dried out from centuries of lying in a salt cave, had turned into a skeletal torch. Jana shivered with primeval fear and hauled Jacob up to the gun port.

Gun port.

Gun.

Gunpowder.

Oh my God.

"Jacob, we need to get out of here right now!"

"Huh?"

"Sorry. No time."

Jana pushed him out of the gun port legs first and hoped for the best.

He landed with a loud thud. Jana jumped out, landing right next to him.

"Ow," Jacob moaned. "Why did you do that?"

"Get up."

Jana hauled him to his feet and helped him walk away from the pirate ship, having to carry almost his entire weight.

"Mexico," he mumbled.

"What?"

"The chatter I heard." He stumbled again. "One of the pirates was talking about someone named 'F' making a deal with a coyote. Coyote is slang for the people smugglers in Latin America. And Frederico is Mexican."

"So, they're going to Mexico? Why?"

"Not sure. They mentioned—"

A deep boom resonated out from the ship, shaking the entire cave.

"That was the first of the gunpower kegs, come on!" Jana shouted.

Jacob managed to get his feet in working order and stumbled along behind her. They switched on their headlamps to see better. The pirates were gone now. If they had posted a guard at the entrance, they were dead. But if they stayed here, they'd be dead too.

Jana helped Jacob up the steep side of the cave. His movements were still uncoordinated, his head hanging.

Another detonation rocked the cave. She glanced at the *Vengeance* and saw a gaping hole had been blown out of the front of the forecastle. It wouldn't be long before more of the old gunpowder lit. Age had probably weakened the powder, or the explosions would be a lot worse, but they helped fill the cave with smoke. Every inhalation made them cough.

They ascended the slope up to the crawlway, Jana having to almost pull Jacob along. Another detonation rocked the air, a bigger one this time. The shockwave knocked Jacob down and nearly sent him tumbling back to the bottom of the cave.

"Only a little farther," she told him, helping him up.

Somehow, they made it to the narrow fissure leading to the cliff face. Jana went first, guiding Jacob as much as she could. Both were coughing constantly now, trying to suck in oxygen that only turned out to be tainted with smoke. Jacob reeled and stumbled, bashing his head against the roof of the fissure and his shoulder against the side. Jana had no idea how he was going to get up the rope.

That worry vanished, replaced by a more serious one.

When she got to the opening, gratefully breathing her first lungful of fresh sea air, she found that the rope was gone.

"Damn it!" She peered up the cliff and saw no sign of it. "The pirates pulled up the rope after them. Jacob, I'm going to have to climb up and get help."

"I can't make it," he moaned, lying on the floor of the fissure, smoke curling around him to make it look like he was emerging from a hole to hell. "I'm sorry, but there's no way I'm getting up that cliff."

"I'll go alone. Don't worry, I'll come back."

"Call Mauricio."

"That scumbag?"

"That scumbag is resourceful and will do anything for money. The CIA has deep pockets. Call him."

Jana hesitated. Mauricio had given her his number, "Just in case you get lonely." As much as she loathed the guy, she realized Jacob was right. There was no time to lose. He'd come and get them and slap a huge price tag on his efforts.

She made the call, hoping the pirates hadn't set an ambush up at the top of the cliff.

CHAPTER TWENTY FOUR

That evening, Jacob rested in the back of a private jet footed by the CIA field station. Mauricio had fetched them from the cliff—the pirates had vanished—and promptly presented them with a huge bill for his services. Jacob felt like throwing him off the cliff but didn't have the strength. Besides, in this game, you never knew when someone like Mauricio would come in handy.

Reece blew his top when he got the bill, and the IOU for Néstor, but after a lot of convincing, he paid up. It took a while to get him to believe the whole story, and he even had an agent interview Néstor and his daughter to corroborate the parts they'd witnessed.

At last, Néstor had warned the field station in Mexico City, gotten them both some much-needed first aid, and loaded them on a plane.

Now, Jacob and Jana dozed in the comfortable seats of the private jet as the lights of Caracas receded below them outside the window.

The intercom came on, and they heard the captain say, "The flight to Mexico City takes seven hours. You have a call from the field director. I'll patch it through."

A TV screen on the back of the seat in front of him came on. Arnold Reece, looking as formal as ever in a jacket and tie, sat in his office. "Hello, Agent Snow. Are you feeling up to snuff?"

"Not really," he replied, wondering what snuff had to do with it. He touched the fresh dressing on his right wrist. His wrist had swelled to the size of a baseball, and he couldn't use the hand at all now.

"I won't keep you long, and then you can get some rest. Have Ms. Peters sit by you. I wish to speak to her as well."

Jana moved over next to him.

"Hello, Ms. Peters. You have been a great help in all this. I never had the honor of meeting your late father, but I'm sure he would have been proud."

"Thanks," Jana mumbled.

Reece went on. "Our field station in Mexico City has alerted the Mexican authorities. They didn't tell the Mexicans the whole story because they were afraid that they wouldn't take the threat seriously. Instead, they told our allies in Mexico that they had good intelligence that a terror group led by a Moroccan planned to set off a bioweapon on Mexican soil. The borders are being monitored, and there is heightened security at all busy areas."

"The chatter I heard between the captain and one of his men mentioned 'tourist central'."

Reece nodded. "We relayed that information. The field station and the Mexican government agree that probably refers to someplace in Mexico City, since that's where most tourists pass through. The airport is being especially monitored, as is the national museum and the national cathedral. Anywhere large numbers of people gather. All the resorts are on alert, too, and their security has been backed up with local police."

"Good," Jacob said, not really feeling reassured. Mexico was a large country, and there were a lot of tourist sights.

While the Mexican police had a bad reputation for corruption, especially when it came to dealing with the narcos, they could be relied on in a situation like this. The CIA and the Mexican secret service had successfully performed more than one anti-terror operation that never made it into the papers.

The real problem was Mexico's border, which to the south—the mostly likely ingress for the pirates—was mostly thick jungle, not to mention sea access on both coastlines.

"Have you alerted the governments of Guatemala and Belize?" Jacob asked.

"Yes. They're on board. They've beefed up security."

"Good. I hope we get there in time. We have a lot of prepping to do."

"The pirates won't get to their destination for quite some time," Reece said. "They have to make it through all of Central America, cross the border, evade the authorities on both sides, and make it to their target. That might take days, assuming they don't get caught."

"These guys are resourceful."

Reece smiled. "So are we, Agent Snow. Now go to sleep. You need it. Perhaps by the time you land, this will all be over."

The screen went black.

"This isn't over, not by a long shot," Jana said, rubbing her bloodshot eyes.

"I agree, but Reece was right about one thing. We need to get some rest. I have a feeling we have some more fighting to do."

152

Jacob popped a couple of painkillers, closed his eyes, and fell asleep instantly.

***

Mounir Zerhouni knew he should get some sleep, but it was hard to sleep when he would soon make history.

He sat in a cramped seat of a sixteen-seat Cessna flying, with its lights off and its transponder removed, low over the jungle so as to escape detection by radar. The *coyote* was good, the best Frederico could find. Mounir trusted Frederico's judgement. The Mexican had been a *coyote* himself once, shuttling immigrants across the hazardous waters of the Caribbean before deciding to try his hand at piracy. Frederico knew his people as well as Mounir knew his own and had found a *coyote* who could be trusted.

Of course, the only thing Mounir trusted about the man flying the plane was his greed, but that was good enough. Greed was something Mounir understood. Greed ran the world, from the greed of the big shipping companies who would rather pay a million dollars in ransom than lose a shipment worth five million, to the greed of the Arabs who had made his own people, the Berbers, second-class citizens in their own country and erased their history.

But greed was not the only thing that moved men. Oh no, he had grown up in a tribe with an ancient warrior tradition. Honor was a motivating force, too, as was vengeance.

The men who he had picked to join him on this cramped and uncomfortable flight were all greedy, but their greed was overcome by larger emotions.

Frederico, for example, wanted to strike back at the cartels who had killed his brother. Gregor wanted autonomy for his people, a little-known ethnic minority in Russia. Aziz wanted the Gulf Arabs sitting fat and rich on an ocean of oil to share more of their God-given wealth with their Muslim brethren.

Mounir wanted liberation for his people.

Every passenger in this plane had a reason greater than greed motivating him, and every man he had chosen for this flight would risk his life for that motivation.

And it was a huge risk, a gigantic roll of the dice.

If it paid off, though, it would go down in history as a resounding victory over the great powers that thought they ruled over the world.

153

200 years from now, a little Berber boy would sit at the feet of his village storyteller and listen to the courageous feats of Mounir Zerhouni, just as he had listened to tales of the courageous Berbers of the old times.

Pretty soon, Mounir would be more than just a pirate. He would be a liberator of his people.

Everyone in this plane had dreams like that. His crew was made up of more than simple thugs willing to brutalize the innocent to gain wealth. They had all become criminals because the system had forced them into it, and they all yearned to change that system.

Not so much because they wanted to become respectable citizens, Mounir thought with a smile. They all liked being pirates but hated the fact that they had no choice but to live a life of crime. And they wanted options for their people.

They wanted freedom, the same as the rich Western nations claimed they wanted for everybody.

Well, now those Western nations would have to deliver. And his own government and those rich oil barons in the Gulf would have to deliver as well.

After the recent pandemic, the world had become terrified of a second one. It had caused so much economic havoc, even among the rich countries. All it would take would be a credible threat, a grand gesture on television and online, and the governments of the world would be lining up to give them what they wanted.

Mounir ran a hand over the duffel bag on his lap. Inside, wrapped among clothing for extra cushioning, was the padded chest Sebastián de Ulloa had put the glass sphere in all those years ago. In the pocket of one of the shirts wrapped around the chest was a printed list of demands. Once they had their hostages, they would release this list to the world.

That list would be an inspiration for all the oppressed people around the globe. Full equality for the Berbers. An annihilation of the cartels that caused misery for the common folk of Latin America. The Gulf states must donate twenty percent of their oil and gas revenue to development projects in poorer Muslim nations. Autonomy for Gregor's people.

And so much more.

It was daring, but even more so, it was just. The powers in the globe would not only concede to the demands out of fear, but because so

154

many of their own citizens would rally in support of those demands. He and his men would be heroes.

For once, they would be in control.

Mounir's chest swelled with pride.

Then he slumped a bit, his brow knitting.

Maybe. Maybe, in their infinite greed and arrogance, the great powers would say no and find a way to take them out.

Then all it would take would to be to smash the glass sphere in the middle of a group of international tourists, and the Black Fever would spread to all corners of the globe.

If they could not have justice, if they could not have freedom, then they would have vengeance.

CHAPTER TWENTY FIVE

Jacob woke as the jet's wheels touched the tarmac. He had slept the entire flight straight through and hadn't even woken up when someone had buckled his seatbelt and put a blanket over him. Jana?

Blinking at the bright morning light of Mexico streaming in through the window, he stretched, his mind already alert. Jacob wished the rest of him was a hundred percent. His neck was stiff, every muscle seemed to ache, and his right hand could barely make a fist. He hoped the authorities could head off those pirates, because he felt pretty sure he wouldn't survive another fight.

A yawn made him turn. Jana, sitting in the opposite row, was struggling out from under a blanket.

The captain came over the intercom as the jet slowed to a stop. "A major from the Mexican army is coming out to meet the plane. I'll refuel and stand by here if you need me. Good luck."

They both got up and went to the door, which was just popping open, the ladder deploying automatically. Jacob was aware that he and Jana both still smelled of the smoke from the burning pirate ship, with a fair amount of B.O. mingled in. The major would just have to deal with it. They didn't have time for a shower.

Stepping onto the tarmac in the private landing area of Mexico City's airport, they heard the rush of jets over on the public side, separated by a chain link fence topped with razor wire. A 747 was just taking off, taking a few hundred tourists back to wherever they came from. Another plane dwindled into the distance, and as Jacob looked around, he saw more planes taking off and landing.

A perfect place to spread disease.

A camouflaged Hummer drove up to the plane and stopped. An older Mexican man with a moustache stepped out, wearing the uniform of the Mexican army. A pistol hung at his belt.

"Hello," he said in English. "I am Major Pedro Obregón of the Mexican armed forces. I will be your liaison during this operation. My orders are to help you in any way I can. It is an honor to work with two CIA agents who are fighting to protect our nation."

Jacob glanced at Jana, who thankfully kept her poker face.

156

"Thank you, major," he said.

"Would you like me to take you to a hotel? You must be hungry. I can arrange a change of clothing as well."

Jacob smiled. "I'm afraid you'll have to put up with our smell until we catch the pirates, major."

"Pirates? I thought they were terrorists."

"They're both. Let's go to the historic center and check out the security measures."

"As you wish, agents. I know a good burrito stand on the way where we can pick you up some breakfast."

They got into the back seat of the Hummer. A corporal at the wheel gave them a nod. Major Obregón got in front, picked up a small bag, and handed it back to them.

"I'm authorized to lend you two pistols. In the bag you'll also find shoulder holsters and spare magazines. Plus, a pair of light jackets to hide them under. A bit warm today for them, but I think it's a good idea."

Jacob opened the bag, his right hand twinging just from the effort of unzipping it. Inside, he found a pair of German-made Heckler & Koch P7 pistols. They fired a 9mm round from an eight-round magazine. Compact with an almost snub nose, they were good for urban combat and weren't the best at long range. Firing with his off hand, he wasn't going to try to take on anything past a couple of dozen yards anyway.

"Any word from our friends?" Jana asked, taking one of the guns.

"No. Our border patrols have picked up several groups of immigrants being led by coyotes, but we haven't come across anyone suspicious."

"They're coming," Jacob said. "They might be here by now."

"There's no way they could be," the major said.

"They had several hours head start on us," Jana said.

Major Obregón chuckled. "Yes, but you came by private jet. They will have to come overland or by ship."

Jacob looked out the window at all the planes. "I wouldn't be so sure."

The major was partially right. Coyotes usually took illegal immigrants on overland routes. But wealthier clients paid more sophisticated people smugglers to take them by air, often to hidden landing strips in the jungle.

The pirates could have gotten to Mexico hours ago. They could have released the Black Fever already.

157

Any one of these planes could be filled with a deadly contagion.

***

Munching on a delicious burrito, his third, Jacob looked around the Zócalo, Mexico City's immense main plaza. He stood close to the city's cathedral, a grand stone edifice with two ornate bell towers and a huge entrance that streamed with visitors going in and out. A metal detector had been set up at the doorway, and policemen were checking bags.

Around the plaza, he saw plenty of security, both military and police, but he also saw countless tourists and locals.

"They haven't cleared the area?" Jana asked, reflecting his thoughts.

Major Obregón shook his head regretfully. "If it was up to me, we would have gone into lockdown. But the politicos ..." He ended his statement with a shrug.

Jacob sighed. He had seen this so often before, both in the United States and abroad. The intelligence services come up with important information, and the politicians, worried about votes and money, don't commit to sufficient security measures. He could practically hear the conversation in the presidential palace on the other side of the plaza.

"We don't even know if these terrorists are in the country yet. They could arrive today, tomorrow, or next week. What are we supposed to do, shut down every tourist site until we find them? Impossible. The police will find them anyway. Maybe we can catch them quietly. No one will ever have to know."

So typical.

"Tourism central, that's what they said," Jacob muttered.

The major nodded. "That could describe any one of a hundred places in Mexico."

"Yeah. But maybe there's someplace special. Someplace different ..."

Jana snapped her fingers. "The jade masks!"

Major Obregón went pale. "You might be right."

She turned to him. "Are they on display yet?"

"The grand opening was last week."

"What are the jade masks?" Jacob asked.

"A set of jade funerary masks discovered at Teotihuacan a few years ago. They came from some nobles' graves there. The best ever found. They made headlines."

"And the museum at Teotihuacan just opened an exhibition about them," the major said.

"The museum must be packed!" Jacob said. "Where is this museum?"

"Teotihuacan is an ancient site about an hour's drive from here," the major said. "The museum is right inside the site, on a road connecting the pyramids of the sun and moon."

Jana looked grim. "A road called the Avenue of the Dead."

"Damn. We got to get there right now!"

"I will call ahead," the major said, already pulling out his phone. "And I can get a helicopter to take us there. We can be there in fifteen minutes."

"That might be fifteen minutes too late."

CHAPTER TWENTY SIX

Jana tried not to get distracted by the archaeological wonderland all around her and focused on the crowd they passed through, looking for the familiar faces of the pirates.

She didn't spot any, but how was she going to spot them in this vast sea of international visitors in an archaeological site that took up eight square miles? This was one of the biggest cities of the ancient world, with an estimated population of 125,000 at its height and a size to match.

Most likely, they'd be in the central part of the site where the best remains stood, and most likely, they'd be at the museum, where she and Jacob headed right now.

The Avenue of the Dead stretched for more than a mile, forty yards wide and ending in the Pyramid of the Moon. To one side along the avenue rose the breathtaking sight of the Pyramid of the Sun, greater in volume than the Great Pyramid at Giza. Smaller stone buildings flanked the avenue, and literally thousands of people were strolling along and taking pictures.

Among them walked plainclothes officers. Jana could pick them out because they were the only ones not looking at the pyramids.

"We're almost there," the major said. The young corporal walked by his side, a submachine gun hanging from his shoulder, scanning the crowd like the rest of them.

"I know the way," Jana replied. "I think it's best if you split up with us. That way, we won't stand out so much."

"The pirates will recognize you."

"They won't be expecting us. They think we're dead. Hopefully that will help us blend in with the crowd."

The major looked them over. "You're the only two people here who look like they've taken a beating."

Jana smiled. "We're also the only people here wearing jackets to hide our shoulder holsters, other than your plainclothes officers. We'll just have to hope for the best."

Major Obregón nodded. "Very well."

He and the corporal peeled off and walked parallel to and a little behind them on the other side of the avenue.

"There's the museum, up ahead," Jana said. Off to one side, set back a bit from the Avenue of the Dead between two stone platforms decorated with bas-reliefs of serpents and ancient gods, stood a low, concrete structure with large, glass windows. Just like at the cathedral, armed guards checked everyone going in.

Jana scanned the crowd. She didn't see any of the pirates, but she hadn't gotten a good look at all of them. Some could be right next to her, and she wouldn't know it.

The museum stood only a hundred yards away. She turned back to study the entrance.

Just in time to see it blow up.

An explosion tore apart the security checkpoint, blasting half a dozen police officers and twice as many civilians into the air.

Even from this distance, the shockwave was enough to make Jana stagger back.

For a second, everyone stared in shocked silence.

Then chaos rippled through the crowd. People began running away in a massed panic, and it was all Jana and Jacob could do to keep from getting trampled.

Through the rush of screaming people, she could see the flaming remains of the museum entrance. Bloody victims lay writhing on the ground or not moving at all.

What she didn't see, to her surprise, was the pirates rushing in.

"They're already inside!" Jana said.

This got confirmed when a pair of uniformed police officers came running up to the museum and got gunned down by automatic fire through the smoke-filled entryway.

"Damn it! What do we do?" Jacob asked.

"There's a back way. A staff entrance I came through the last time I visited a colleague here."

"Won't that be locked?"

"We'll shoot the lock."

"They'll hear."

"Hopefully not over their own firing."

Jana led them around the building to a back door next to a loading dock. The door was steel and looked strong. Jacob pulled out his gun, the movement awkward as he tried to draw with his left hand from a right-handed holster, stood to one side, and fired at the lock.

The door swung open.

Just ahead of them, a man swung around, an UZI coming level with their gut.

Jacob took him out with a single shot to the head.

Beyond the body, they saw a hallway with several side doors ending at another closed door. For a moment, they stood to either side of the entrance, but no other pirates appeared. Scattered firing continued inside.

"Let's go!" Jana said.

They rushed inside, guns leveled, and checked out each of the side rooms, several offices and a lab, all abandoned.

"They've already taken hostages," Jacob whispered. "Damn. These guys work fast."

"Must have had a contact on the inside," Jana whispered back.

They advanced down the hallway, guns leveled. They heard more shots from somewhere in the building, muffled by distance or closed doors.

The hallway ended at a door. If Jana remembered right, then that door led to one of the public display rooms. She heard shouts and crying on the other side.

They were only a few steps from it when it opened.

A lean Southeast Asian man with a submachine gun walked through and stopped, eyes wide, surprised to find people in a wing of the building he thought he'd cleared.

Two bullets punctured his skull simultaneously.

No more time for stealth. They rushed up to the doorway and looked past.

Beyond was a display room full of pottery painted in the garish colors and elaborate figures of Mesoamerica. On the floor cowered a group of Mexicans, Asians, and Anglos. An Arab came rushing into the room with a sawed-off shotgun. Jacob fired, winging him in the shoulder. The pirate staggered and fired back, but his aim was off, and he demolished a display case next to the door.

Jana took him out with her next shot.

"Take that submachine gun," Jacob said, "and put your pistol in my holster."

Jana did as he asked. He couldn't use anything that took more than one hand.

A megaphone rang out through the tiled halls of the museum.

"Stop firing!" a man demanded in Spanish. By now, Jana could recognize the voice as belonging to Mounir. "I have in my possession a bioweapon. If you make any attempt to stop us, I'll infect every one of the hostages. The museum is full of people. I estimate at least three hundred. They will all die of a rare disease for which only I have the cure."

Jana and Jacob traded a look. That last part was a bluff. No one had a cure to the Black Fever. But the police and army surrounding the building didn't know that.

"Stop firing," Mounir demanded again. "I have a printed list of demands. I will send one hostage out with this list. You will broadcast this list on all channels the Mexican government owns, post it on your government website, and relay it to all embassies. The officers who have infiltrated the building will lay down their arms immediately."

Jana and Jacob traded another look. They hurried over to the crowd of hostages and lay face down on their weapons, hoping they wouldn't be spotted in the crowd.

A sunburned American tourist stared at them with wide eyes.

"You're going to get us all killed," he whispered.

Jana glared at him. "If you narc on us, I'll kill you myself."

The American buried his head in his hands.

The sound of boots on tile. Jana dared a peek.

Three pirates entered, bearing pistols. They looked around, confused for a moment, then rushed to the open door.

A few tense moments of waiting. Two came back.

"They fled outside," one called over to the far room. "Aziz is guarding the doorway."

Mounir sauntered into the room, holding the orb in his hands. Jana hid her face.

"Good. Double check all the rooms to make sure they're secure and then we'll send a kid out with our list of demands. Gregor, you go and …"

His voice trailed off. There was a tense silence. Feet shuffled. A bolt snapped back. Feet approached.

Someone grabbed her by the hair and pulled her head up.

One of the pirates grinned down at her. Another had his gun in her face. A third covered Jacob.

Mounir chuckled. "Wow. I am impressed. Careful now, don't make a move. Guys, check them for weapons."

Jana and Jacob slowly began to rise, revealing the weapons they had been lying on.

Just as a hailstorm of bullets came from the door leading to the staff area.

The corporal who had driven them here rushed in, firing away with his submachine gun. He took out all three of the men standing over Jana and Jacob before Mounir whipped out a pistol and shot him through the head.

Another pirate rushed in from the next room, only to get taken down by Major Obregón as he ran in at the same time. Mounir shot at him, missed as the major ducked to the left, fired again, and hit him in the leg. The major fell, slamming his head against a pillar. He didn't get up.

"Watch it!" Mounir shouted, holding the orb high.

Jana and Jacob dropped the guns they had just picked up.

His words got nearly drowned out by the sound of firing in the front of the museum.

"Stop firing!" he shouted at his men. "Stop firing!"

"They're coming through!"

Mounir looked around, panic engraved on his features.

"This wasn't how it was supposed to be," he moaned to himself in Arabic. "It was supposed to be controlled."

Jana summoned up the courage to walk toward him.

"It's over," she said in Arabic. "If you give up now, you won't be put to death. Spare these people and spare yourself."

Mounir looked her in the eye, and what she saw in those eyes frightened her more than anything she had seen on this mission.

"And be a nobody? Never to have my name in history?"

He wound up like a baseball pitcher and threw Ulloa's glass sphere at the wall.

Jana was already intercepting. She leapt in the air, extending her body, reaching for the sphere.

Her fingers wrapped around it inches before it hit the wall.

She twisted her body and landed hard on her back. The impact sent a jarring pain through her entire body. The sphere slipped from her fingers, pinked on the hard tile, and rolled away.

Mounir ran for it.

Three quick shots rang out. Jacob had gotten into the action. Mounir jerked and stumbled back, his chest punctured in three places.

He looked down at his bloody shirt. Gunfire still echoed in the rest of the museum but was already dying down. They heard shouts, calls for surrender.

"It wasn't supposed to be this way," Mounir said. "I was supposed to go down in history."

Jacob fired once more, this time hitting him between the eyes.

Jana scrambled for the sphere.

"No. Oh, no. I can't believe I dropped it."

It might be her going down in history as the archaeologist who set off a global plague because she dropped a historic artifact.

She picked up the sphere, squinted at it, turned it every which way.

Not a single crack.

Jacob came up, "Is it …?"

"Good quality glass." Jana said and laughed, hearing the cutting edge of hysteria in her laugh.

Major Obregón groaned and sat up.

"Why did you rush in?" Jana asked.

"It wasn't me," the major said, gesturing at the corporal's body. "It was Corporal Escarra. He panicked. He has a niece who was supposed to come here today with her school group."

"He died a hero," Jacob said.

The major shook his head. "Poor man. He just got engaged."

A dozen heavily armed men rushed in, Mexican police and secret service.

"We have the bioweapon," the major told them. "Is the building clear?"

"Yes," one of the plainclothesmen said. "The terrorists who weren't killed have surrendered. None of the hostages died."

"Good," the major said, looking woozy as he clutched his bleeding leg. "I'm going to need to go to the hospital, though."

Jana held the sphere, the cause of so much trouble, not daring to move.

Jacob turned to her.

"We'll get the bomb squad to take that."

Jana nodded. She had gone as rigid as a statue. Probably best considering the circumstances.

Jacob turned to look at Corporal Escarra.

"Poor guy," he whispered. "He probably knew he wouldn't make it out. He sacrificed himself for family. Reminds me of someone else I once knew." He turned back to Jana. "After the bomb squad takes that sphere off our hands, there's one more thing we need to do. Well, one more thing I need to do."

"What's that?"

He looked back at Corporal Escarra again. "I think it's time I told you the truth about your father."

CHAPTER TWENTY SEVEN

They sat on a bench in one of the rooms of the museum. All the civilians had been evacuated, guards secured all entry points, and they were alone except for the jade faces of long-dead nobility watching them with stoic expressions.

Jacob paused. Now that he finally relented and promised to tell Jana the truth, he'd grown afraid. He'd rather fight another band of pirates than go through with it.

But there she sat, gazing at him, hoping to hear something that would fill in the gap her father had left in her life.

He doubted he could do that, but at least he could give her closure.

Taking a deep breath, he just let it come out. "I went AWOL in Afghanistan. My Ranger unit went crazy and started a massacre, something as bad as Mai Lai in Vietnam. We were all under pressure, out in the middle of nowhere and seeing our guys get killed, but that's no excuse. The others went crazy, and then I went crazy too."

Jana went pale. "You took part in a massacre?"

"No. I stopped it and perpetrated a massacre myself. I killed some of the guys in my unit. Most of them, actually. I just snapped. Seeing them do those things ... I couldn't ... We were supposed to be the good guys. I had to stop them. Then I ran off. Went feral." He stared at the floor, no longer having the strength to look her in the eye. "I hid in the mountains, killing Taliban, coalition forces, local tribesmen, anyone who came after me. Then someone came after me I couldn't stop."

"My father."

Jacob nodded.

When she didn't say anything, Jacob went on, "Aaron Peters, your father, managed to capture me. Succeeded where entire platoons of Taliban and the U.S. Army failed. He took me in, helped me heal. I was ... institutionalized for a time. Your father pulled a hell of a lot of strings to keep me from going to jail for the rest of my life. He saw I had potential and managed to convince the higher-ups to use that potential instead of waste it."

"So, he got you into the CIA?"

"I could never go back to the military. They're too strict to ever consider it. The CIA, though, play a little more fast and loose."

Jana crossed her arms. Jacob looked up at her and saw she was frowning. "You could put it that way."

"I know we have a bad reputation, and I'm not saying we haven't done some bad things in the past. But for the most part, we defend the West against threats. You've seen that for yourself. We need a flexible organization that will deal with misfits in order to do our job. You think the military would have ever done business with Mauricio? Or even Néstor? No. In the hidden battles, the more important battles, there are no rules."

"Like the rule that says a father's place is with his daughter."

Jacob looked down again. "I'm sorry he picked me over you."

"I beg your pardon?"

"He became like a father to me. Guided me. Mentored me. Led me on my first missions."

"He wasn't your father, he was mine!" Jana shouted so loudly that a Mexican soldier popped his head through the doorway. She waved him off with an angry gesture. The man looked from Jana to Jacob and back again, then shrugged and disappeared.

"He was both of ours. We went on several missions together."

"And cookouts and birthday parties," Jana said, obviously fuming.

"I needed that. You needed that too. He couldn't be in two places at once, and he chose the wrong place. He was a great man, but he wasn't perfect. Dad raised—"

"Don't call him that!"

"Aaron raised you to be independent, and I guess he figured you didn't need him as much as I did."

"Idiot," Jana muttered.

Jacob wasn't sure if she meant him or Aaron. Maybe both.

He went on. "The last mission was in ISIS territory. In the early days, just as they were getting big. We in the CIA saw the threat long before the White House did. So, Aaron and I went in to blow up a central munitions storage they had in Raqqa. We wanted to make it look like there was resistance within the Islamic State by other groups. There wasn't, but we hoped we could turn a lie into a truth."

"Typical."

"We infiltrated via the desert, blended in among the foreign fighters, and then hit the ammo dump one night. That's when it all went sour. They might have been crazy, but those ISIS fighters aren't stupid.

They laid a trap for us. Aaron sent me to fight my way out, saying he'd join me once he'd rigged the place to blow. What I didn't realize was that he didn't have enough fuses. He had to set it off by hand."

"By hand?"

"The ammo dump needed to go, so he sent me out to save myself, not telling me he couldn't join me. I almost didn't make it anyway. The explosion took out an entire city block. Killed dozens of ISIS fighters."

"My father became a suicide bomber."

Jacob's head snapped up. "Don't call him that. He died a hero!"

"How many civilians were in that city block?"

"None. It was a base for fighters."

"How can you be sure? Did you take a census?"

"Of course not. But we did scout the area. Look, I thought you wanted to know how Dad died."

Jana leapt to her feet. "He wasn't your dad, and he wasn't mine either!"

She stormed away. The soldier looked into the room again and got shouldered aside as Jana went out. By the time Jacob made it to the doorway, she was gone.

He paused in the empty museum, his head hanging.

Opening up to her had been a mistake.

He had lost Gabriella, and now he had lost Jana.

***

Jana ignored Jacob's shout for her to wait, ignored the police and the staring crowd. All she wanted was to get away from Jacob, get away from his lies, and get away from everything to do with the CIA.

She was going home. Reece down in Caracas had given her some money and an emergency passport. She'd go to the hotel the Mexican government had provided and arrange a flight back to the United States. The CIA could pay for it. No, better if she asked the Mexicans to. She didn't want to owe the CIA anything.

Even though they owed her so much.

They owed her a family. They owed her a childhood.

She walked down the Avenue of the Dead until she got to the main entrance. A police cordon stopped anyone from getting in or out, but one of the officers recognized her and let her through. She moved to the parking lot outside.

A taxi driver standing next to his car waved at her.

169

"Taxi, Miss? Where you go?" he asked in broken English.

"Anywhere but here," she said, getting in the back.

"What?"

"The Azteca Hotel. It's downtown."

"I know this hotel. Very good place."

The driver got the taxi into gear and nosed his way through the crowd.

"Big trouble at Teotihuacan?" he asked, looking in his rearview mirror at the chaos.

"Yeah."

"Narco fight?"

"Something like that."

They got out of the parking lot and onto a main road.

"I live in Cuidad de Mexico but come here for fares. My daughter, she go to school here."

"That's nice." Jana said, her arms crossed and staring out the window. She didn't feel like chatting right now and hoped the guy would shut up.

"She get out of school now. Oh, there she is!" He pointed to the sidewalk, where a group of girls about twelve years old stood, all holding bookbags. They wore blue skirts and sweaters as a school uniform. "May I pick her up? She save money for the bus."

Jana softened. The girls reminded her of Eva. "All right."

The driver came to a stop in front of the girls. A young woman about twenty years old pushed through them and got in the front seat.

Jana sat up straight. "This is your daughter?" The driver didn't look old enough to have a daughter in her twenties.

The woman pulled a pistol from her purse and stuck it between the two front seats, aiming right at Jana's midsection.

"No, I'm the woman who will kill you if you try to escape, Jana Peters."

Jana looked around helplessly. The woman kept the gun low and out of sight. No one on the sidewalk reacted.

The back doors on both sides opened, and a man came in each one.

"Just keep calm and you won't get hurt," one of them said.

"Who are you? Are you with the pirates?"

The driver chuckled and switched from broken English into fluent English. "If only you were so lucky, Ms. Peters. I'm afraid you've fallen into far, far worse hands. But don't worry, it's not you we're after. You're just the bait."

170

The taxi merged with the traffic, drove for half a mile, and got onto the highway heading out of town.

EPILOGUE

The Pamir Mountains, northeast Afghanistan near the Tajikistan border
Three days later ...

Operative 313 was hunting again.

Online chatter relayed to him via one of the region's monitors via a satellite phone he kept at one of his many caches of equipment had led him here, north from the Khyber Pass and across the length of Taliban-held territory to the far edge of the country.

The chatter had picked up what might be an operative of The Order working with local tribesmen dissatisfied with Taliban rule and who were organizing resistance. That resistance, fortified within this vast range of snowy peaks shining with blinding brightness in the sun, was beginning to gain momentum.

That should have made Operative 313 and his superiors happy. After all, according to the old Sanskrit proverb, "The enemy of my enemy is my friend."

While that was true in most cases, it was never true with The Order. They were up to something, something that would hurt the West and its democracies. Despite their name, they wanted to sow chaos. Just what their ultimate goal was remained a mystery.

So, Operative 313 had ordered a satellite hack and trace on the enemy's sat phone and pinpointed it to a small village in one of the region's lush valleys. The valley was broad and green, nourished by a wide stream of icy water. Fields of wheat, barley, and millet waved in the wind, and herds of cows grazed on rich grass. What a contrast to the barren, rocky slopes at higher altitudes and the frozen wastelands farther up than that.

He had observed the village at a distance, hiding amid the stalks of grain and having to move several times to avoid farmers working in their fields and young boys sneaking away to catch a couple of precious hours of play time in days that were otherwise filled with relentless toil. This was a hard land, and children worked almost as much as adults. Survival required that it be so.

He had spotted his rival operative easily enough, a broad-shouldered man who, at a little over six feet, towered over the diminutive frames of whipcord muscle that typified the people here.

For a day and a night, he watched, until at the crack of dawn the next morning, the man from The Order left.

That's when Operative 313 started his hunt.

Up through a narrow gorge on the side of the valley, both hunter and hunted avoided the village boys tending flocks of sheep and goats, up and up past the last of the scraggly grass to a jagged-toothed ridge and over onto a vast plain of boulders scattered like marbles by some infant titan.

Operative 313 lost sight of his quarry there, but the man's goal was obvious. Due east lay a pass into a series of other valleys claimed by a different tribe. Because they were neighbors, these two tribes were natural enemies. Every now and then, Operative 313 came across old shell casings, mute testament to the frequent skirmishes that broke out in this barren No Man's Land.

Operative 313 kept after him, weaving through the boulders and keeping a bit to one side of the route he guessed the man from The Order had taken, checking every corner in case of ambush. While he didn't think he'd been spotted, it paid to be careful.

That guy should remember that. He was being sloppy. Not only had he used an older code the CIA had hacked a year ago, but he had also stayed in that village long enough for Operative 313 to track him down.

Maybe they were getting too confident. With all the trouble happening around the globe, and with the Western allies having pulled out of Afghanistan like so many great powers had pulled out before, maybe this guy thought he was safe.

Operative 313 would show him just how wrong he was.

But the hunted wasn't the one to get a nasty surprise. It was the hunter.

Rounding another boulder in this vast maze of glacial detritus, Operative 313 spotted an open space, a dry riverbed a quarter of a mile wide.

And there, at the opposite bank, leaning with arms crossed against the flat face of a rock, stood his quarry.

Spray painted in big red letters on the rock was the name, "Aaron Peters."

Operative 313's heart sank to his knees.

The man from The Order did not see him for a minute, and in that minute, Operative 313 assembled his sniper's rifle. Then, with a sharp eye trained from years of fighting, his quarry raised his hand and waved as if to an old friend.

He called out in English with an American accent, "Agent Peters! If you shoot me, your daughter, Jana, will die."

Operative 313's finger eased off the trigger. His quarry grinned and strolled over to him. Operative 313, codename for Aaron Peters, kept the man in his sights. His enemy from The Order seemed unconcerned.

Once he got to within a hundred yards, Peters called out, "That's close enough!"

The man might be bluffing, trying to get close enough to detonate a suicide vest. That wasn't The Order's style, but the CIA and its allied agencies knew so little about the shadowy organization that Peters wasn't going to take that chance.

"Agent Peters, I have some news for you."

"Agent Peters died years ago."

"No, he didn't. He's right here. You've been difficult to track down, Agent Peters. So has your daughter. But we have her now. My superiors sent me some photos. I have them on my phone. I'll show you those in a minute."

"If you've hurt her, I'll—"

"She's just fine. If you want her to remain fine, you'll do exactly as we say."

"What do you want?"

"First off, if I don't call my superiors within twenty-four hours, she'll be killed. If, during that call, I don't confirm with some photos that you've been captured, she'll be killed. If you try to escape, she'll be killed. Have I made myself clear?"

Aaron Peters lowered his rifle. "You have."

The man chuckled and walked closer.

Aaron growled, "If you think I'm going to talk, you're mistaken."

"You'll talk. We're keeping her until you do. Now put that gun down. The long fight is over, my fellow warrior. A bigger one is coming. But it's a fight we're going to fight, not you. Your time has passed. The time of the entire West is passing."

Aaron Peters gave his rifle a regretful look, then stepped out of cover   with   his   hands   up.

174

NOW AVAILABLE!

TARGET FOUR
(The Spy Game—Book #4)

"Thriller writing at its best... A gripping story that's hard to put down."
--Midwest Book Review, Diane Donovan (re Any Means Necessary)

"One of the best thrillers I have read this year. The plot is intelligent and will keep you hooked from the beginning. The author did a superb job creating a set of characters who are fully developed and very much enjoyable. I can hardly wait for the sequel."
--Books and Movie Reviews, Roberto Mattos (re Any Means Necessary)

From #1 bestselling and USA Today bestselling author Jack Mars, author of the critically acclaimed *Luke Stone* and *Agent Zero* series (with over 5,000 five-star reviews), comes an explosive new action-packed espionage series that takes readers on a wild ride across Europe, America, and the world.

Archeologists are found murdered in the wake of discovering a mysterious, precious relic, deep in the jungles of South America, and Jacob Snow, elite soldier-turned-CIA agent, finds himself in a race against time to uncover the mysterious motives. Not only is this ancient relic priceless, but it could unsettle world security.

Jacob knows he must turn once again to his mysterious partner and archeologist to help decode the riddle. Who would kill for a mythical object, and why?

Can they stop the terrorists—and prevent a global disaster—before it's too late?

An unputdownable action thriller with heart-pounding suspense and unforeseen twists, TARGET FOUR is the fourth novel in an exhilarating new series by a #1 bestselling author that will make you fall in love with a brand-new action hero—and keep you turning pages late into the night. Perfect for fans of Dan Brown, Daniel Silva and Jack Carr.

Future books in the series are also available!

Jack Mars

Jack Mars is the USA Today bestselling author of the LUKE STONE thriller series, which includes seven books. He is also the author of the new FORGING OF LUKE STONE prequel series, comprising six books; of the AGENT ZERO spy thriller series, comprising twelve books; of the TROY STARK thriller series, comprising five books; and of the SPY GAME thriller series, comprising six books.

Jack loves to hear from you, so please feel free to visit www.Jackmarsauthor.com to join the email list, receive a free book, receive free giveaways, connect on Facebook and Twitter, and stay in touch!

BOOKS BY JACK MARS

THE SPY GAME
TARGET ONE (Book #1)
TARGET TWO (Book #2)
TARGET THREE (Book #3)
TARGET FOUR (Book #4)
TARGET FIVE (Book #5)
TARGET SIX (Book #6)

TROY STARK THRILLER SERIES
ROGUE FORCE (Book #1)
ROGUE COMMAND (Book #2)
ROGUE TARGET (Book #3)
ROGUE MISSION (Book #4)
ROGUE SHOT (Book #5)

LUKE STONE THRILLER SERIES
ANY MEANS NECESSARY (Book #1)
OATH OF OFFICE (Book #2)
SITUATION ROOM (Book #3)
OPPOSE ANY FOE (Book #4)
PRESIDENT ELECT (Book #5)
OUR SACRED HONOR (Book #6)
HOUSE DIVIDED (Book #7)

FORGING OF LUKE STONE PREQUEL SERIES
PRIMARY TARGET (Book #1)
PRIMARY COMMAND (Book #2)
PRIMARY THREAT (Book #3)
PRIMARY GLORY (Book #4)
PRIMARY VALOR (Book #5)
PRIMARY DUTY (Book #6)

AN AGENT ZERO SPY THRILLER SERIES
AGENT ZERO (Book #1)
TARGET ZERO (Book #2)
HUNTING ZERO (Book #3)

Made in the USA
Middletown, DE
29 August 2024

59955715R00109